# Twilight Child

# ALSO BY SALLY WARNER

*Not-So-Weird Emma*

*Only Emma*

*A Long Time Ago Today*

*This Isn't About the Money*

*Sister Split*

*Bad Girl Blues*

*How to Be a Real Person (In Just One Day)*

*Finding Hattie*

*Totally Confidential*

*Accidental Lily*

*Leftover Lily*

*Private Lily*

*Sweet and Sour Lily*

*Sort of Forever*

*Ellie and the Bunheads*

*Some Friend*

*Dog Years*

# Twilight Child

SALLY WARNER

VIKING

VIKING
Published by Penguin Group
Penguin Group (USA) Inc., 345 Hudson Street, New York, New York 10014, U.S.A.
Penguin Group (Canada), 90 Eglinton Avenue East, Suite 700, Toronto, Ontario,
Canada M4P 2Y3 (a division of Pearson Penguin Canada Inc.)
Penguin Books Ltd, 80 Strand, London WC2R 0RL, England
Penguin Ireland, 25 St Stephen's Green, Dublin 2, Ireland
(a division of Penguin Books Ltd)
Penguin Group (Australia), 250 Camberwell Road, Camberwell, Victoria 3124,
Australia (a division of Pearson Australia Group Pty Ltd)
Penguin Books India Pvt Ltd, 11 Community Centre, Panchsheel Park,
New Delhi – 110 017, India
Penguin Group (NZ), Cnr Airborne and Rosedale Roads, Albany, Auckland 1310,
New Zealand (a division of Pearson New Zealand Ltd)
Penguin Books (South Africa) (Pty) Ltd, 24 Sturdee Avenue,
Rosebank, Johannesburg 2196, South Africa

Penguin Books Ltd, Registered Offices: 80 Strand, London WC2R 0RL, England

First published in 2006 by Viking, a member of Penguin Group (USA) Inc.

1  3  5  7  9  10  8  6  4  2

Text and maps copyright © Sally Warner, 2006
All rights reserved

LIBRARY OF CONGRESS CATALOGING-IN-PUBLICATION DATA
Warner, Sally.
Twilight child / by Sally Warner.
p. cm.
Summary: Taken from eighteenth-century Finland by her father, teenager Eleni
eventually finds a home in Scotland, receiving help along the way from brounies,
fairies, and other creatures she has the ability to see and talk with.
ISBN 0-670-06076-3 (hardcover)
[1. Fairies—Fiction. 2. Orphans—Fiction. 3. Scotland—History—18th century—
Fiction. 4. Finland—History—18th century—Fiction.] I. Title.
PZ7.W24644Twi 2006
[Fic]—dc22
2005023565

Printed in U.S.A.
Set in Minister
Book design by Sam Kim

PUBLISHER'S NOTE

To Mirja Kivistö,
my dear Finnish friend
and honorary sister–*kiitos*

# Contents

## Prologue
### TWILIGHT CHILD ✳ 1787

## Part 1
### A FAIR COUNTRY ✳ 1793

## Part 2:
### THE HEART OF THE WORLD ✳ 1793–1794

# *Epilogue*
## NEW SCOTLAND ✳ 1794

# Twilight Child

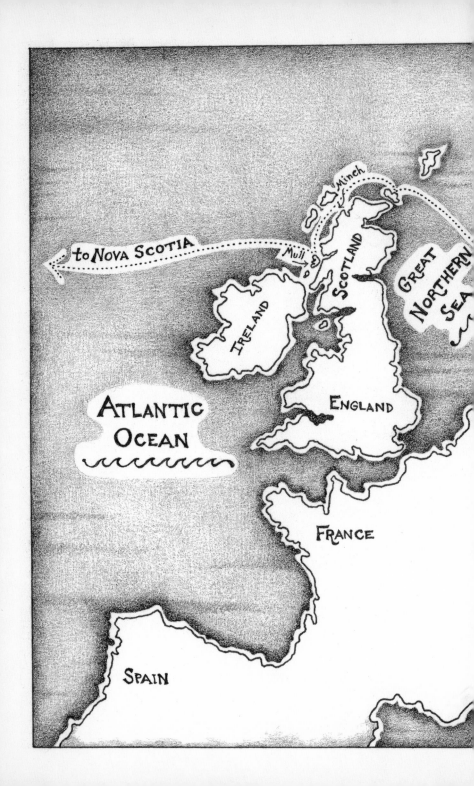

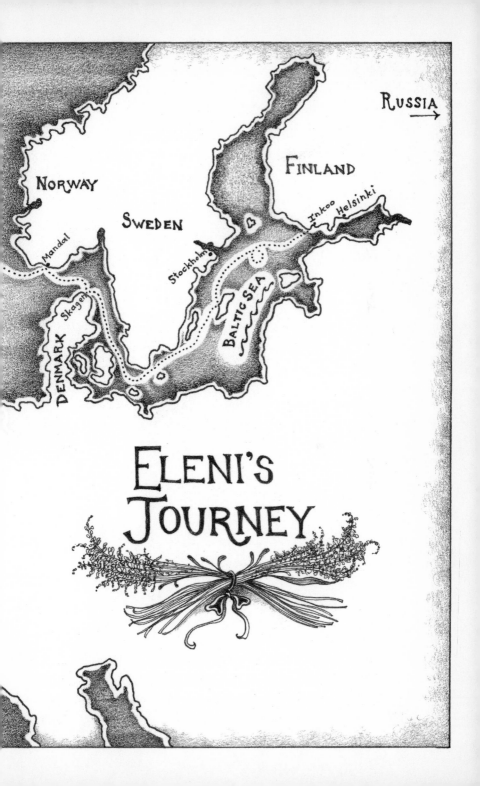

RUSSIA →

NORWAY

FINLAND

SWEDEN

Helsinki
Inkoo

Mandal

Stockholm

Skagen

BALTIC SEA

DENMARK

ELENI'S
JOURNEY

# 1787

# Twilight Child

"'A Russian is a Russian even if he's fried in butter,'" Eleni called out, quoting one of her father's favorite Finnish sayings. "Isä says." She laughed as she lifted the heavy white-blonde braid from her neck to let the cool forest air touch her skin.

"Huh," Matias said, not turning around.

Eleni's *äiti* and *isä*—her mother and father—were eating a farewell dinner with Matias's parents now, she knew, or sharing a sauna, or swimming, or drinking, or doing whatever it was parents did before reluctant fathers left to fight a war.

Of course, Matias's father was a shoemaker by trade, Eleni reminded herself. He was a nervous, indecisive man, and her own father was a quick-to-anger fisherman, so certain his way was best that men seldom worked for him longer than a month or two. Neither wanted to be a soldier, but what choice did they have? They had been ordered to join the army.

The parents would call for Eleni and Matias to come home soon, Eleni knew, but for now, they were free to roam the forest behind their homes in Inkoo, near Finland's southern shore.

"Isä says, Isä says," Matias grumbled without looking back as he stepped carefully over a tiny, stripped-bare blueberry bush. "Don't try to act so grown up, Eleni. You are just an infant! And of course we should not trust the Russians. But we should not trust the Swedes, either."

"Even though our fathers are willing to go fight their wars for them?" Eleni asked in her softest voice.

"Even though," Matias said firmly. "The Swedes are our masters, and they mean to do Finland no favors. They only want to use our army to defeat the Russians—so they can become even richer. That's what war is, Eleni."

"I *don't* trust 'em, then," Eleni cried, hoping to please the boy—eleven years old, already, while she, Eleni, had only just turned nine. She reddened, feeling a little ashamed of being so young.

"Keep moving, baby Eleni," Matias teased over his shoulder, and Eleni struggled to catch up with the boy, who was striding through the forest as if he owned it. Matias was not afraid of the most powerful woodland spirit, Eleni told herself, awed. Or of the tallest ant hill, or the fiercest brown bear, or the biggest moose. Not that a shy, bumbling moose would come anywhere near such a ruckus as she and Matias were making. And bears were seldom seen this close to the village of Inkoo anymore, and Matias had nothing to fear from forest spirits—when he was with her, anyway.

Eleni knew this. She blushed again. "I am not a baby," she told Matias. "And you are not a grown man, so don't tell me what to do in my own forest!"

Matias whirled around to face her, and his summer-brown face was twisted with pain or anger, Eleni couldn't tell which. "But our fathers *are* grown men," he cried. "Should they not have a say in the course their lives are to take? And will I ever have a say in *my* own life?"

Eleni stepped back onto a crunchy sprawl of gray reindeer moss, her heart thudding. For if the army did claim Matias for its own some day, then his dream of becoming a healer—a bone-setter, a gash-stitcher, a fever-soother—would vanish like the first autumn snowflake falling on the nearby Baltic Sea.

"We are nothing but beasts of burden to our Swedish masters, Eleni—and in our own land, too," Matias said, still angry. "Why should that be so?" he asked, as though he was really expecting her to answer.

Eleni almost tingled, trying to come up with a reply Matias would admire, but she could not think of anything to say. And so without warning, she flung herself onto his back—just as she had when they were younger.

"Get off! Wretched little pest. Don't you *dare*," Matias said, twisting this way and that as he tried to swat Eleni off his back.

Furious and thrilled, Eleni clamped her legs even tighter around Matias's narrow waist as the handsome boy tried to dislodge her. "I hate you to pieces," she cried, pinching his strong thin arm as hard as she could.

"Witch! Twilight child!" Matias shouted, knowing what would hurt her most.

He had heard the stories, of course.

But then suddenly he was laughing, and despite his taunts,

Eleni started laughing, too. "Don't you dare, don't you dare," she chanted, teasing him, although she no longer thought about the words she was saying.

"I do dare," he said, whirling around once more. But Eleni would not be moved.

And so Matias stood still while Eleni held on tight. She could hear the forest breathe.

Eleni had seen three kinds of forest spirits—at different times, of course, since the creatures preferred to live alone—near this very place. She saw a tiny *keijukainen* when she was only four years old, the enchanting flying creature who could make a person's dreams come true. Eleni was so thrilled by this unexpected encounter, however, that she forgot to make a wish. "Little bird!" she had cried. The *keijukainen* seemed to shake with silent laughter before flitting deeper into the forest.

Eleni had seen the ugly *peikko* trolls three times in the forest over the years, but after the first time, the experience did not frighten her much. The forest was where these gentle beings lived, but if she didn't eat too many of the autumn mushrooms they adored, and if she moved softly, keeping to the forest's web of ancient and improbably narrow moose trails, Eleni knew, the *peikko* would leave her alone.

She saw the much-feared *menninkainen* only once, when she was seven years old, but she knew instantly this larger being, the most revered—and feared—forest spirit of them all, did not mean her any harm. *"Twilight child,"* he said, almost growling, and he lifted a large, gnarled hand in cordial greeting.

"What does 'twilight child' mean?" she had asked her mother that night.

Äiti had been combing Eleni's tangled hair, but she paused, surprised by the question. "Why?" she asked, instantly wary. "Where did you hear those words, Eleni?"

"From the creature in the forest," Eleni said, and Äiti's hands clutched at her daughter for a moment, then fell into her lap, helpless.

"Oh," the woman said, breathless for a moment. "Well, daughter," she began slowly, "it has long been said that when a baby is born at twilight, the precise moment that hangs between day and night, that child is given a special gift. She is able to sense other in-between things in this world as well."

"Please, no," Eleni said softly. "That cannot be true."

"It should not surprise me," her mother said, not hearing Eleni's words. "For not only were you born at twilight, daughter, but it was *Juhannus,* midsummer, at the end of the longest day of the year. And that one night is only minutes long, here in Finland. I suppose this means that your gift will be all the greater, my child. I had not known for certain you possessed it, though."

"But—but I do not want that gift, Äiti," Eleni said, her green eyes welling with tears. "We must give it back at once!"

"We cannot," Äiti told her, stroking Eleni's hair with some sadness—and looking at her only child as if with new eyes, Eleni realized, horrified.

"I want to see only what you and Isä see," Eleni had said.

She was weeping, although she did not know why.

"Are you *crying* back there?" Matias asked Eleni, craning his neck in the attempt to get a look at her face. He sounded disgusted.

"No. I was thinking, that's all," Eleni said, resting her head against the flat back of Matias's patchwork vest, so carefully pieced together by his father from soft scraps of leftover leather. The vest was far too big for Matias, but it felt warm, and Eleni loved the way it smelled.

"Well, stop it," Matias mumbled, shifting his legs a little. "I am not going to carry you home, you know," he announced suddenly. "If that's what you're waiting for."

"I don't want you to carry me home," Eleni said, much offended.

"Then get down," Matias told her. He sounded very stern.

"I can't," Eleni said. "You'll chase me if I get down."

Matias didn't argue, because it was true.

And so they stood there together, almost alone in the gently breathing Finnish forest, and they waited for someone to call their names.

# $\mathcal{P}$art 1

# A FAIR COUNTRY

# 1793

*"Finlande is called a fayre Countrye. . . ."*

George North

From *The Description of Swedland, Gotland, and Finland*

Originally printed by John Awdely, London, 1561

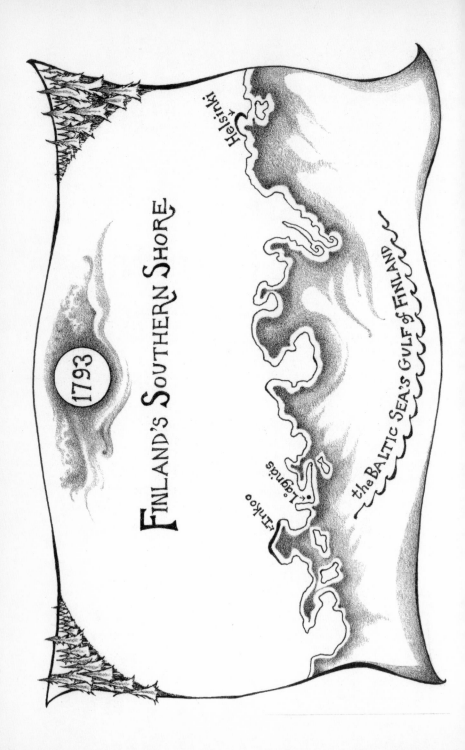

FINLAND's SOUTHERN SHORE

1793

Helsinki

Inkoo

Lagnäs

the BALTIC SEA's GULF of FINLAND

༄༅༅༄

# Chapter One

# Washing Sigrid Wallibjörn's Feet

"**M**y feet are sore, *flicka*," the Lady Sigrid told Eleni, stretching her plump white legs winningly in the girl's direction. She was perched on her chair's richly embroidered cushion like a child, Eleni thought, though the woman must be well over forty. She was old, anyway, and her two sons were grown and had fled back to Sweden, and her husband, Svendgard Wallibjörn, often journeyed to Stockholm on business, leaving her alone in Inkoo.

The woman spoke in Swedish, of course, not the Finnish that almost-fourteen-year-old Eleni and her parents had always spoken together. But Eleni had learned to comprehend her mistress's languid words over the past few years.

Few Swedes ever bothered to learn much of the Finnish tongue, but then, why should they? It was difficult, and they were the rulers.

Eleni tried not to splash the hot water she was pouring from the pitcher to the wide earthenware bowl in preparation for washing Sigrid Wallibjörn's feet. "Don't burn me, now, or I'll have to strike you," Lady Sigrid said in her half-teasing way.

"And you know I hate it when you make me do that," she added, closing her eyes.

"I know, *Fru*," Eleni murmured, unafraid. She sprinkled lavender buds into the water and then leaned forward to breathe in the fragrance, musky and sweet.

Eleni had last been slapped by her mistress almost two years ago, shortly before she turned twelve. She'd sneaked away from the Wallibjörns' house on a warm summer's morning in an attempt to visit her mother, who had just begun working at Lågnäs, a few miles away. Lågnäs, just east of Inkoo. The farmhouse there was desperate for a cook, and they did not mind—though others had—that Eleni's mother was the wife of a now-vanished rebel.

Eleni's mother was still well, then.

But Eleni had been spotted trudging toward Lågnäs along the wide dirt road that led from Inkoo to Helsinki, through forest, field, and more forest, and she'd been scooped up like a shivering rabbit and brought back to Inkoo in the back of a rattling hay wagon. The Lady Sigrid had been more frightened than angry when she struck her, Eleni remembered.

She dabbled her fingers in the water to test how hot it was, and judged that by the time she'd counted to ten five times, its temperature would be perfect. She and Lady Sigrid waited in silence by the flickering fire.

"*Ohhh*," Lady Sigrid said with a sigh when Eleni placed the woman's feet in the bowl and began rubbing them gently. "I was on my poor trotters all day, trying to teach the new maids how to do things correctly. Why, they are nearly wild! They know nothing of town ways."

"*Ja*. You are right about that, *Fru*," Eleni said mildly, calming her. She rubbed her thumbs in small circles on the Lady Sigrid's tender arches, hoping to make the woman jump a little—or at least laugh.

But why, Eleni wondered suddenly, why *should* the new maids know anything of life in an almost-grand Swedish household? They were the country-bred daughters of men who had been happy to farm or to forest the trees or, farther north, to herd reindeer—until those men had been called into service by the ever-hungry army and their families scattered throughout the land. For the Swedes' war against Russia raged on, though in more muted form since the rebellion, and Finns were still caught in the middle.

"One girl crossed knives on the table at the midday meal, which any civilized person knows is to invite bad luck," Lady Sigrid said, continuing her complaint. "And the newest girl— the fattish one—put her dusting cloth on my Bible. Right on top! Have you ever heard of anything so blasphemous, Eleni?"

"*Nej, Fru.*"

"Thank goodness you were raised a town girl," the Lady Sigrid said, sighing her relief. "You are most pleasing to look at, and you have such a delicate way about you that you could almost be a lady. And yet you are not afraid of hard work. It makes things so much easier for me," the woman added, and her blue eyes filled with self-pitying tears.

"*Ja, Fru*," Eleni murmured, rubbing harder now.

"Ouch. Be gentle, *flicka*," the Lady Sigrid said, pulling her foot back a little. "You should not have left me this afternoon," she said suddenly, remembering.

Eleni did not reply.

Frowning, the Lady Sigrid reached for the plate of fragrant *pulla* that had been baked for her by one of the wild girls, and the tantalizing smell of cardamom filled the air. Eleni's mouth filled with water as her mistress bit into the sweet bread. "I needed you, Eleni," Lady Sigrid said, aggrieved.

Eleni stifled a sigh and stroked her strong fingers along the bottoms of the Lady Sigrid's wet feet, making the woman's toes curl like shrimp. "I had to go into the forest, *Fru*—to gather goat willow bark for my mother's special tea. I visit her tomorrow, remember? You promised that I could."

Lady Sigrid shifted uneasily on her cushion, for in truth, she did not like the idea of Eleni visiting her mother one bit. "But all the willow tea in the world has not helped her fevers yet, *flicka*," she began gently.

"It eases her discomfort a little," Eleni said. "And it might help her tomorrow."

If only Matias were here to tell her how to heal Äiti, Eleni thought, biting her lip. But her old friend and his mother had melted into distant Helsinki's crowded streets after the rebellion. Matias was rumored to be working for a shoemaker there.

She missed him.

Lady Sigrid tried another argument. "You cannot be of any help to your mother if you become ill, too, Eleni," she said. "And I do not want you to bring any noxious vapors from the sickroom at Lågnäs into this house."

"I will not, *Fru*," Eleni said, stifling a sigh—for after all, Äiti was not spreading her illness even to anyone at Lågnäs, as far as Eleni could tell. Not that folks there seemed worried. They firmly believed that Eleni's mother was pining—wasting away, really—for her vanished rebel husband. That was their explanation for her illness.

The way Eleni understood it, her father and the others in what was now called the Anjala League had conspired—though supposedly fighting in the Finnish army *for* the Swedes—to cause Sweden's bloody campaign against Russia to fail some five years earlier. Because why, Eleni's father asked his fellow soldiers, should Finland always have to be the reeking, bloody battleground in the struggle between Sweden and Russia? And why must more Finns be slaughtered merely to prolong Swedish rule over beautiful Finland?

What did they owe the Swedes?

Although the conspiracy had failed, its perpetrators either killed, as Matias's father had been, or fled, like Eleni's father, Sweden's thrust east toward Russia was greatly weakened by these men's acts.

Eleni was secretly proud of her father, for Finland had changed with the rebellion—if only a little. Bold folks in town hummed old tunes the Swedes once had rolled their eyes at, for instance, and servants were not so quick to stop speaking Finnish when their masters came near.

"And I want you to pray before entering the house, when you return from Lågnäs," Lady Sigrid said, bringing her own white hands together as if to show Eleni how it was done.

"I always do, *Fru*," Eleni lied.

"The toes now," Lady Sigrid murmured, waggling them playfully in the cooling water.

Eleni stifled a sigh and went to work as instructed. The Lady Sigrid's toes were red with bumps and gnarled with hidden calluses, but Eleni kneaded them with her fingertips until her mistress sighed with pleasure.

Lady Sigrid would be off to bed soon, Eleni knew—after sampling a few more *pulla,* perhaps. The woman yawned like a cat. "You will be tired and upset when you return from Lågnäs, *flicka,*" the woman murmured sleepily, worried in advance.

"Mmm," Eleni replied. Lady Sigrid did care about her at least a little, she admitted to herself. But she also knew that Sigrid Wallibjörn's real concern was for her own comfort. After all, Eleni knew her mistress's ways, and her touch was tender, and she never burned even the finest woven lawn with the small, heavy irons the Lady Sigrid liked used for crisping every ruffle and pleat.

Lady Sigrid yawned again. "I am tired, Eleni. I am getting old," she said, looking sad.

"*Nej, Fru,*" Eleni lied again. How strange to become old, yet wish to be told you were the same as always, Eleni thought as she helped the thick, clumsy woman into her sleeping gown and tied her bonnet beneath her chin.

But Eleni was almost fond of the Lady Sigrid in many ways. Lady Sigrid had gone to some trouble to make sure that little Eleni was warm enough at night when she had first come to this house at age nine, aching for her mother, worried about her father, missing Matias, and so frightened that she thought she might wet herself if anyone scolded her or asked questions about her family.

And the Lady Sigrid was generous with sauna time on

Saturday night. Her husband had wanted to tear down the small smoke sauna—the *savusauna*—saying it was dangerous, so near the house. But he really shared the growing Swedish belief that saunas only led to immoral behavior among the Finns.

"I won't hear of tearing it down," his wife had said. "*You* are not the one who will be stuck here with a houseful of moping Finns every Saturday night, Svendgard Wallibjörn. And you can trust me to see they behave themselves," she added.

Lady Sigrid knew already such watchfulness would not be necessary, for the Finns prided themselves on behaving in the sauna as they would in church.

"It's not right," her husband said, scowling.

"Why interfere?" his wife asked, making her final—and most compelling—appeal. "It won't cost you as much to keep the sauna as it would to hire a new batch of servants every month!"

And so the sauna had stayed.

"My best coverlet, *flicka*," the Lady Sigrid instructed Eleni, after placing herself so carefully in her bed that it looked as though she were practicing for eternity. "It is mild outside now, but the poison chill will settle in before morning, no matter how firmly my shutters are closed and my curtains are drawn."

"*Ja, Fru,*" Eleni said, lifting the soft, padded throw from the gaily painted wooden chest that held it—and others almost as fine. She floated the coverlet across her mistress's bed and then turned to go. "May Jesus be with you this night, *Fru*," she said, pausing at the door as she repeated the blessing the woman had come to expect.

"Thank you, Eleni. And my own prayers are with your mother, child."

The next morning, Eleni's step lightened as she walked away from the main road and headed down the rutted path that led to the earth-red farmhouse at Lågnäs. A cloudless blue sky stretched above her, and the distant forest surrounded her like the rim of some gigantic wheel.

The forest watched her, Eleni knew.

Snaky lines of smaller, softer trees crisscrossed the vast fields around her, revealing the locations of the streams and rivulets working their way toward the nearby Gulf of Finland, part of the Baltic Sea. A raucous mob of black-and-white oyster-catchers—their red mouths gaping with frantic cries—tumbled toward a patch of freshly tilled earth in search of worms.

The dirt was warm beneath her feet, and Eleni paused to work her toes into a soft patch that felt as though it had been ground as fine as the cake flour at Lindstrom's mill, back in Inkoo. Although she was anxious to see her mother, Eleni paused to turn in a slow, complete circle, her arms out-stretched. She relished both her temporary freedom and the warm morning. "Beautiful," Eleni whispered, breathing deep.

She would stay the night at Lågnäs, and there would be sauna after the evening meal. Äiti could not help but feel better in its sacred heat.

And when she and her mother had breathed the healing steam and baked so hot that their skin almost quivered, and when every worrisome thought had vanished from their heads, the strongest servant at Lågnäs would carry her mother back to the farmhouse, and Eleni would settle her mother back into bed. Then she would run through the twilight, down the narrow path leading to the rock—as wide as a fine Swedish room—that sloped into the half-briny, half-sweet sea.

And in she would plunge!

Water grass would tickle her legs then, and she would look up through the water at the fading light of a precious summer day.

And then that day would be over forever.

# Chapter Two

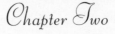

# Good-bye

"*Good-bye, twilight child,*" a hoarse voice whispered from the shadows inside the *savusauna,* and Eleni awoke with a start.

The feeble light coming from her lantern, which hung on a hook by the door, seemed to shudder for a moment. There were only two other sources of light in the windowless log-house structure behind Svendgard Wallibjörn's house: the sliver-thin cracks in the old wooden door, and the one small opening in the sauna's ceiling. But neither light revealed the speaker.

The wooden ladle in Eleni's drooping hand clattered to the floor. It was late Monday night, only one day after her return from Lågnäs, and two days after the Wallibjörn household's usual Saturday night sauna. But the remaining water in the room's small barrels was still warm, and a faint heat continued to radiate from the sauna's charcoal-encrusted walls. Longing for both peace and privacy, Eleni had slipped away just before bedtime to wash.

"Tonttu, is that you?" she asked, matching the voice's whisper.

She had not seen him in more than a year, although the Wallibjörns' sauna was the only place on this earth the little creature was bidden to watch over.

A shadow shifted slightly behind the *kiuas*, a raised, oven-like structure in the center of the room. The loose stones inside would still feel hot if she touched them, Eleni knew, but heat never bothered the *tonttu*. He loved it. *"Yes, it is I,"* the *sauna-tonttu* finally said, as if having given the grammar involved in his reply some thought.

"Where have you been?" she asked, reaching for her shift—although she knew that the little *saunatonttu* would never gawp at her nakedness. He was too proper—almost prudish, really!—for that, and besides, Eleni thought, smiling a little, of what interest would a mortal maiden be to such a one as he?

And yet this *saunatonttu* had made Eleni aware of his presence almost from the day she had been taken in as a housemaid by Sigrid Wallibjörn. He called her "twilight child," as if he knew.

*"I have been here,"* Tonttu said. *"And not here, when he was here."*

And Eleni knew at once to whom the *tonttu* was referring, because these guardians of the sauna—smaller than the *peikkos* in the forest, and much smaller than the *menninkäinen*—were widely known to hate drinking, cursing, and loud noises of any kind. And Svendgard Wallibjörn certainly supplied all three things when he was at home in Inkoo.

"But that man has not been in Inkoo for almost twelve weeks, Tonttu," Eleni said. "His business in Stockholm keeps him away," she added, hoping that the *tonttu* would not think she was arguing.

*"Feh! I could still smell his stink,"* Tonttu said, sounding disgusted.

"Really?" Eleni asked, fascinated.

*"Of course, really,"* Tonttu exclaimed from behind the *kiuas. "I am very sensitive, child. And why would I bother to speak these words if they were not true? Although I do like to talk. To you, anyway,"* he added, as though determined to be honest with Eleni—however painful or embarrassing to himself this might be.

Eleni made no reply, but she was certain the *tonttu* did not expect one. As far as she knew, she was the only person in the household who had ever heard him speak—or, indeed, who knew for certain that this creature really existed. Almost every Finn had old tales to tell of such sauna spirits' interventions, however: the drunk's period of unexpected bad luck; the helpful, pious lad's sudden tremendous good fortune; the young woman's surprisingly easy delivery of twins upon the *savusauna* platform, that clean, warm place where most Finnish babies were born.

But Tonttu had not spoken to Eleni more than five or six times in all, as she was seldom alone in the sauna.

Perhaps he was lonely! The thought startled Eleni, and it also saddened her.

*"Do not be sad,"* Tonttu said firmly, as if he knew a little of what she was thinking. *"That man will not be coming here again."*

"Oh, Tonttu, but he will," Eleni told him, for she did not want the small timid creature to become too disappointed when Svendgard Wallibjörn—dragging with him all his various revolting smells—came bursting back into their lives, as he always did.

"*He will not,*" Tonttu repeated firmly. "*On his journey home to Inkoo, Svendgard Wallibjörn collapses and dies before his boat sails past the last of Sweden's islands.*"

"Tonttu," Eleni cried, greatly shocked. "Are you telling me that he has already—"

"*He* will *die,*" the *tonttu* corrected her. "*Unfortunately, he is still among the living.*"

"But—but—but—"

"*Butbutbut,*" the *saunatonttu* repeated, gently mimicking her. "*You and I cannot save him, child. Ahti has already claimed him.*"

Ahti, the god of the deepest seas!

"But—but Tonttu, Svendgard Wallibjörn is a *Lutheran,*" Eleni said, as if hoping that might change things.

The *saunatonttu* surprised Eleni by making a sound she had never heard before. It was a combination of snow squeaking, of wind sighing through Baltic reeds, and of cold water hissing when it hit the *kiuas*'s heated rocks on Saturday night.

The little creature was laughing! "*Tonttu,*" Eleni exclaimed, almost angry with him.

"*Do not scold, twilight child,*" the *tonttu* said after catching his breath with a series of wheezes. "*It is not I who determined his fate, and I cannot save him.*"

"And yet you know these things," Eleni said, frightened. Poor Lady Sigrid! What would become of her if this indeed were true? Ever since Saturday night, Eleni had been scheming how best to ask the woman to release her to go work at Lågnäs—at least until Äiti's health improved.

But now, the Lady Sigrid would need her here in Inkoo more than ever before.

"*I know these things,*" the *saunatonttu* agreed, sounding both sad and smug. "*It is simple, really, because the future is not so very different from the past. You cannot lay a finger upon either one, after all.*"

The darkened sauna was silent for a moment. "But Tonttu," Eleni finally said. "Even if Svendgard Wallibjörn is to die, why must you say good-bye? He will never disturb your peace again. You needn't leave this place."

"*I am not leaving, twilight child. You are,*" Tonttu told her.

Eleni's heart seemed suddenly to swell with joy. *Lågnäs!* Tonttu must know she would be granted permission to go care for her mother.

"I will miss you, Tonttu," Eleni said, wishing more than anything that she could gather the shy little being into her arms and embrace him.

"*I will miss you, too,*" he told her, seeming to shrink back a little. "*We will never see one another again, my child. There will be other twilight creatures in your life, however. And you know you have the gift to see them.*"

"But—but *why* do I have that gift, Tonttu?" Eleni asked, her eyes searching him out in the gloom. "Was I chosen for it, or was it given to me only because I happened to be born the exact moment that I was? And what am I supposed to do with my gift?"

"*I do not know why you are a twilight child any more than I know why I am a tonttu,*" Tonttu said, shaking his head. "*I think other children might have the gift, too, could they stay quiet long enough to hear the voices of our world. As for what you are to do with your gift, why, perhaps you are meant to protect the twilight world, or to tell its story. But I do know your gift means you will never be alone."*

"Of course I won't be alone," Eleni said, laughing. "You will always be here, Tonttu. And Lågnäs is not *so* far away! I'll come visit you when my mother is better."

*"Never again, never again,"* the *tonttu* said firmly, and he retreated farther behind the *kiuas.*

Eleni knew this meant it was time to take her leave of him. "You have been a true friend to me, Tonttu. *Kiitos,"* she said, thanking him.

The *saunatonttu's* shadow disappeared entirely. *"And now I will have no one to talk with,"* Eleni heard him say to himself.

"Good-bye," she said softly.


One week later, just after midnight, Eleni was dozing on the thickly padded mat that lay in front of Lady Sigrid's big kitchen fireplace, her coverlet pulled around her like a cloak. The weird between-light of a northern midsummer's night seemed to fill the room like water. It was dark enough, however, for the few embers left from last night's fire to cast their rosy glow upon the blue-and-white tiles decorating the inside of the fireplace. It would be her job to stoke that fire to life for breakfast, Eleni knew, but the chore was hours away.

She was not asleep, but neither was she fully awake. Instead, Eleni thought, she was trapped in twilight—like the girl in the ancient Finnish poem, the one whose life felt strange to her because she was always alone.

For she *was* alone, Eleni told herself sadly, in spite of what Tonttu had said.

Eleni did not hear the kitchen door open an hour later, its iron lock no match for an intruder far craftier than any thief the locksmith at Inkoo could have anticipated. A man entered the Wallibjörns' vast kitchen without making a sound, and he stared across the gloom at the girl who lay sleeping by the fire.

Her back was to him, and she was curled up like a kitten. Tears gleamed amid the man's whiskers.

*"Eleni,"* her father whispered.

# Chapter Three

# Leaving Finland

Eleni shivered, crouching low in the small boat her father's man rowed. The coverlet from the Wallibjörns' house was still wrapped around her, but it was heavy with sea spray now, and it provided scant warmth.

As the silent sailor rowed, Eleni watched her father—who was staring not at her, but back toward Inkoo harbor. The sky was light enough that she could see the fierce blue of her father's eyes, narrowed though they were against the wind. He was crying, and Eleni had never before seen him cry—or any man, other than Inkoo's simpleton, Simo.

"Are we going to go get Äiti?" she asked, shouting to be heard. But her father did not reply.

Disturbed, and frightened by this new, strange Isä, Eleni turned to watch Inkoo get smaller and softer as dawn mist rose from the summer-warm water of the Baltic Sea. The village of Inkoo had curved trustingly around its small harbor on the southern shore of Finland for more than four hundred years, Eleni knew, having grown up hearing the stories. The Vikings themselves once sailed close along these forested shores as they headed east to plunder vast, unknowable Russia, pausing to raid little Finland as they went.

Her father seemed like a pillaging Viking to her now. Had he not stolen her away?

When she was only a thistle-haired toddler, Eleni remembered suddenly, shivering, she sailed with her father—a gentle Isä, then—to a nearby place that was widely known to be an ancient Viking burial island. It was recognizable instantly—even from much farther out at sea—because of the gigantic round rock that seemed to guard its southernmost shore. The rock must have been as tall as four grand Swedish houses stacked upon themselves!

"Did God put that rock there, Isä?" little Eleni asked her father as water sloshed against the sides of his old fishing boat.

"That rock was there before God," had been her father's abrupt, mysterious reply. "The Vikings chose the island so they would never lose their dead."

*Never lose their dead,* Eleni thought now, trying out the words. "Äiti is at Lågnäs," she said aloud, frightened to speak—but knowing that she must. "We should be heading east along the coast if we are to find her. We are going the wrong way, Isä." She hardly dared to say it.

"We are not going to Lågnäs," her father said, wiping away the few tears the wind had not yet taken. "We are leaving this place forever, Eleni."

"We are leaving *what* place? Inkoo?" Eleni asked. She tugged frantically at her father's tattered sleeve, but he would not look at her.

"Yes, Inkoo," her father finally said, uttering the words as if they caused him great pain. "And we are leaving Finland forever, too." He turned away, wrenching his gaze from the shore.

"No, Isä," Eleni cried. "We cannot leave without—"

"She is dead, Eleni. Äiti died of the fever at Lågnäs. I was with her at the end."

For one crazed moment, Eleni almost laughed. Dead? Isä was wrong, most certainly! Hadn't the *saunatonttu* promised her that she, Eleni, was to go to Lågnäs to care for her mother until she was well?

*No*, a cold voice within her said. *He told you only that you were leaving Inkoo. And he looked sad, and he said, 'Never again.'*"

"Turn around and face the horizon, daughter," Eleni's father said, snapping out the words. He still spoke without looking at her.

Chastened, Eleni turned away from tiny Inkoo. It was true, she thought, stunned. That was why Tonttu had looked so sad. Äiti was dead.

Eleni stole a glance at her father. Grizzled whiskers seemed to stream from his face like the thickest and wildest sea grass that Eleni could imagine. He looked like Väinämöinen, she thought suddenly—the old sage of the ancient poem who claimed to have helped create the world.

Had her father lost all reason? Eleni wanted to cry, but she was too afraid.

The rowing man slowed his stroke a little, and his oars shifted back in their iron locks with a hollow clatter, and Eleni saw they had at last reached the bigger ship that was their destination.

✺✺✺✺

The Finnish word *Saari* had been carved into the side of the ship—larger by half than her father's old fishing boat—by a practiced hand. "Island," the word meant; though Eleni could not read, she had seen it copied out on old Finnish maps in Svendgard Wallibjörn's library, so she recognized its form. She looked up at the two men's faces staring down at her.

"Stand, girl," her father commanded, and Eleni was half pushed and half dragged aboard the *Saari* like a sack of wet flour. Her coverlet fell behind her and was lost in the vast green sea.

Eleni rolled over the rail and onto the bigger ship with a thigh-bruising thump. She tried desperately to cover her bare legs with the wet folds of her sleeping gown, a thin linen shift that had served also as her undergarment back in Inkoo. Now, she realized suddenly, this clinging gown was the only article of clothing she owned!

"Back away, hounds," her father told the two gaping men, his voice rough. "Akseli, fetch some garment to warm my daughter," he commanded the tall, bony young man who'd been staring at Eleni the hardest, as if she were a meal he would like to eat—making her think briefly of flinging herself over the side of the ship. "And Pekka," Eleni's father continued brusquely, "help Jakob to stow the little boat. And then we will set our sail."

The men went about their assigned tasks without speaking, as if all words among them had long since been used up. The small rowing boat was hoisted alongside the *Saari*'s stern, and its long oars stowed, and a square dark sail was raised swiftly up the bigger ship's mast. The sail was as crazed with mends and patches as Matias's old leather vest, Eleni thought, and unlike any she had ever seen.

Matias!

She was losing him, too, Eleni realized, shaken. He was her only friend, and now he would never be able to find her. For where was her home now that her beloved *äiti* was dead?

As the lonely thought came to her, the *Saari* began to creak slowly through the water. It was as if the ship knew its own mind, or the mind of its master.

*Chapter Four*

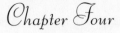

# Swallowed Alive

"I want to go home, Isä," Eleni murmured, half-asleep in the gloom.

Her own voice startled her awake, and Eleni was afraid for a moment her father had heard her plaintive words. But he was not nearby.

*Home.* Eleni bit her lower lip as she thought about the word.

When she was a little girl, home had been a place. It was the little fisherman's cottage in Inkoo. That cottage was cramped and small, Eleni realized now, having served for years in the Wallibjörns' big house, but she had been happy there—so happy, she had never even thought about it!

But she had felt equally at home in the forest behind Inkoo, whether she was with Matias—dear Matias, wandering fatherless now through Helsinki's busy streets—or by herself.

But then their fathers went to war, and there was the rebellion, and everything changed.

After that, Eleni thought sadly, curling tight into a ball atop the crumpled extra sail that served as her bed, home was a person. Home was her mother, who'd lived at Lågnäs for these last few years. "Äiti," Eleni whispered, and she tried not to cry, because her *äiti* was gone forever. There was no one in Inkoo to honor her grave, for that was a daughter's duty.

Eleni tasted the names of the flowers she would put on her mother's grave if she could: *valkovuokko*, the wild anemone; *ruiskukka*, the heavenly blue flower that grew in Finnish rye fields; *lemmikki*, forget-me-nots.

She would *not* forget, Eleni promised herself. Like the ancient Vikings, she would not lose her dead.

Now, Eleni told herself, the only home she had left was within her own memory. And so she closed her eyes and remembered being a very young child getting ready to go for a sail on her once-gentle father's fishing boat.

She remembered being nine years old, and clinging to Matias in a Finnish forest.

She remembered nestling in her mother's arms at Lågnäs.

She remembered everything.


The *Saari*, a crude cargo ship, was pointed at both ends. It was about fifty feet long and fifteen feet wide, but it was so shallow that a person always had to crouch when under its rigid cover. There were only three men other than Eleni's father onboard. All were Finns, Eleni quickly learned: the frightening Akseli; Pekka, a fair-haired boy from the north with tilting-up eyes; and Jakob, the silent rower, who was almost as old as her father.

Inside the ship, the biggest space was in the middle, and this space was covered by narrow beams and cloth that was so stiffened by tar, it was nearly as hard as wood. It was dark underneath this reeking protection, and it was often so wet there the sailors had to bail water.

In this one large space was crowded whatever cargo the ship carried, even young animals; the casks of fresh water that kept them all alive when they were at sea; the smaller casks of grog, which were counted and guarded by the men as if they were gold; and the barrels of salt fish and hardtack bread that was their nourishment each day. No cooking was ever done onboard the *Saari*, for any open flame could quickly prove fatal aboard a wooden ship.

The men who were not working the sail rising above the waterproof covering, or manning the *Saari*'s heavy steer-board, which was on the right-hand side of the boat, Eleni quickly learned, slept in this crowded central area alongside the cargo. A triangular space at the rear of the boat was separated from the central area by a flimsy wall made from the rotting boards of shipping crates long since fallen apart.

This space was reserved for Eleni's father, the captain of the ship, and now for Eleni, too. In fact, she was banished to this cavelike chamber almost all day, being allowed to crawl above and blink at the sun only when her father was watching her— and keeping an eye on his men, who seemed half wild and were not accustomed to having a female on the ship.

Eleni knew she distracted the men from their work, so she tried to make herself useful to her father by performing those small domestic chores the men did not have time to do. She mended their tattered clothes, and she patched the extra sail where it was torn.

But why, Eleni wondered, had her father taken her from

the Lady Sigrid's home? And why did he so often turn his head away as if he could not bear to look at her?

Isä *had* loved her once, Eleni told herself. She remembered falling asleep upon his broad chest often, on those seemingly endless summer nights when even the littlest Finnish children were allowed to linger with their elders, watching light play upon the water.

Eleni recalled in particular one *kokko*, the *Juhannus* bonfire out on a rocky island, the old Finnish way to celebrate the ancient holiday. She perched on her father's shoulders and watched the sparks leap high into a violet sky. The world had been a perfect place then, and she was at home in it.

As the days passed, Eleni discovered she truly hated being at sea. There was no peace aboard the *Saari*. No longer silent, the men bellowed and cursed throughout each day, and sometimes young Pekka cried. The sail flapped, and always there was the sound of water whispering against the *Saari's* pitch-caulked, overlapping planks.

It was as if she'd been swallowed alive by a great fish, Eleni thought, shivering.

There was no way other than by using her fingers for Eleni to comb her hair, which was growing matted and dull with saltwater, sweat, and tears, and soon she was no longer able to braid it, it had become so tangled. And so she fashioned a kerchief from a ragged scrap of rough fabric too threadbare to be mended, and she tied it tight behind her neck, as if this one small attempt to groom herself properly might be her salvation.

The smell of the ship was almost indescribable. The *Saari* reeked of such foul things as unwashed men, tar, spilled grog, calf mess, and the smell from Eleni's own brimming chamber-pot.

But when Eleni tried one day to wash parts of herself with the small amount of water that was her daily allotment, her father roared his displeasure. "You won't act so finicky and fine when your tongue swells up black with thirst, girl," he said, snatching the bucket of water from her hands and starting to dash its contents into her face. But then he thought better of wasting the precious stuff, and he set the bucket aside.

"I always had enough water to wash myself in Inkoo," Eleni cried, unable to hold back her angry words. "Why did you steal me away from there, if I am to die of thirst on these wide waters?"

Furious, her father stared at her with fierce blue eyes. "You are mine," he finally said. "And a man cannot steal what already belongs to him. Did you think I would leave you alone in Inkoo, now that you have no mother nearby to protect you? Better off dead! Inkoo is no longer your home, daughter. Nor is Finland, not from now on."

"Then where *is* my home?" Eleni asked, shaking.

"It will be in Spain, once we get there," her father said, turning away from her once more. "I know a woman in Spain," he added in what was almost an embarrassed mumble.

Her father knew a woman? In *Spain*?

This Isä was a stranger to her now, Eleni thought, and she felt both furious and frightened.

## Chapter Five

# Pekka Speaks

"Did you always live in Inkoo, *tyttö?* In one town?" young Pekka asked Eleni shyly, almost enviously, as the *Saari* slopped through the Baltic's gentle swells, temporarily becalmed. Everyone was aboveboard, basking in the sunshine of a mild—if windless—day, though Eleni sensed that her father, alone at the ship's bow, was worried about losing precious hours to the lull. But even he seemed somewhat at peace today, knowing there was nothing he could do to change their situation. Rowing would do them little good in this vast central part of the Baltic Sea.

Jakob and Akseli were absorbed in fishing off the side of the ship, although Akseli looked sullenly in Eleni's direction from time to time.

Eleni stole a glance at Pekka. They were sitting near each other in the sun, toward the stern of the ship. Eleni was now wearing one of her father's old shirts and a makeshift skirt she had stitched together from tattered lengths of sacking.

The fair-haired boy was only a year or two older than she,

Eleni thought, although he called her *tyttö*, "girl," as if he were a grown man. But it was hard to tell his exact age, he was so pinched and brown from living at sea. A long white scar traced the turn of one of the boy's scrawny forearms. Pekka's front teeth stuck out a bit, and one of them was broken partway off, making him look even younger than he probably was. But his blue eyes sparkled with an optimism that was difficult for him to hide.

"Yes, I always lived in Inkoo, Pekka," she said, smiling a little. "My father was an ordinary fisherman once, and my mother, she . . ." Her voice faded.

"I know about your mother, *tyttö*," Pekka said, keeping his voice low. "I was with your father at Lågnäs when she died."

"You were?" Eleni asked, surprised.

"Yes. We went several times in the last two years," Pekka said. "Always in the summer, you know—whenever we slipped back to Finland. The folks at Lågnäs did not mind. They kept our secret, and they fed us fine hot food." He licked his lips, remembering.

Eleni stared at Pekka, trying not to let her jaw drop in amazement. Was the boy lying? He did not seem to be. And yet her mother had never said a word to her about these visits.

"It is the truth, *tyttö*," Pekka said, a rising blush making his brown skin seem to glow. "And we saw you, too, in Inkoo. We took the little boat in to shore and hid her in the reeds. Three times in all." He hooked his blond hair behind his ears and smiled.

"You *did*?" Eleni asked, almost squawking her surprise. "But—but—"

"Your father had to make sure you were safe," Pekka explained. "He did not like Svendgard Wallibjörn much, see, but the man was so often away that it did not matter. And the Lady Sigrid was just foolish, but kind enough to you, your father thought. And your mother was not far away, in case anything went wrong."

"Lady Sigrid *was* kind enough," Eleni echoed, still disturbed by the thought of Isä having been so near without her knowledge. But then, her father could not show his face openly in Inkoo, she realized—not with so many powerful Swedes living nearby. And so Isä could not be faulted for having hidden himself from her.

"Your mother held both his hands at the end, and she called out your name," Pekka told Eleni softly. "But she was very calm, *tyttö*, and she did not suffer. She was lucky."

"Oh. Thank you for telling me that," Eleni said, struggling to keep her voice steady.

"Your father, though, *he* suffered," Pekka said. "And so he came for you, to take you away from the Swedes for all time. For they are his sworn enemies."

Pekka seemed really to like Isä, Eleni thought, surprised. For whatever reason, the young man was not afraid of him. "How did you meet my father, Pekka?" Eleni asked quietly.

"It was in Helsinki. He saved me from a beating there," Pekka told her, beaming.

A beating! Eleni gazed out at the water that surrounded them. She wanted to ask Pekka if he had seen Matias in that city, but she knew it was a foolish question. Helsinki was a big, big place, and many people lived there. More than she could imagine, old folks in Inkoo told her smugly.

And anyway, Pekka did not even know what Matias looked like.

Halfway down the length of the *Saari*, Jakob tugged at his fishing line, and Akseli nudged him viciously with his elbow and muttered a few harsh words. Both men looked in Eleni's direction and laughed, taking care that Eleni's father did not hear them.

Eleni shuddered, turned her face away, and closed her eyes.

"When I got to Helsinki, I stole some bread," Pekka said quickly, as if hoping Eleni was not paying too much attention to this part of his story. "And the baker's man chased me. He wanted to punish me, for it is wrong to steal."

"You were just a boy, though," Eleni said, frowning. "And you were hungry, Pekka."

Pekka shrugged. "The Bible does not allow for that when it says we must not steal," he remarked, as if he had given the matter some thought. "But your father was in Helsinki, *tyttö*—hiding in a crowd, as the old saying goes. You know, after the rebellion."

Eleni nodded.

"And he saw the baker chasing me," Pekka continued, "and he paid him for the bread, and he rescued me! He had just bought this ship. Well, with the help of some men who believed in what he and the other rebels had done. And he was getting ready to flee Finland, and so off we went. I was lucky, really." Pekka smiled once more.

"Yes. Lucky," Eleni repeated, without meaning what she

said. For Pekka seemed to think everyone was lucky—no matter what dire thing befell them. Her mother, himself. What terrible event had to happen for a person to be deemed *unlucky* by this sweet but simple lad? "But it's a hard life for you onboard the *Saari*, Pekka," she ventured.

Pekka laughed quietly. "I don't mind the work," he said. "I am glad of it." Eleni gazed out at the horizon. A slight breeze grazed her cheek, and, grateful, she turned her face toward it.

"But it is better now that you are with us, *tyttö*," Pekka said, stumbling a little over the words. "You are a maiden who makes things sweet, and life is different now. You are not only his daughter. You are like a sister to us all."

"Hey! Squirrel Boy," Akseli shouted to Pekka. "Stop chattering like a girl, and come help us fish."

"*Ei,*" Eleni's father called out, shaking his head as he got stiffly to his feet. "You can *both* stop chattering, for the wind has risen. We will be off in a moment, if you can stir your lazy bones. Eleni, you go below."

"He can't risk losing you, see," Pekka whispered as Eleni took a last breath of clean, sweet air.

But it was up to her, and not her father, to see that she survived, Eleni told herself as she climbed back under the heavily tarred cloth. No matter what her father said, she was not his property! And when the opportunity came, she decided that very afternoon, she would escape the small island that was the *Saari*, and its sailors, *and* the stranger her father had become. And she would live out the remainder of her life as an exile, wherever that might be—though not in Spain with some vile foreign woman her father "knew," Eleni vowed silently, angrily.

She would be lucky, too, Eleni told herself—but she would make her own luck from now on.

The *Saari* cut across the now-choppy sea to Gotland, a large island in the middle of the southern Baltic. Eleni almost wept with homesickness, seeing beautiful farms and the island's trees. But when the ship anchored at Visby to pick up its cargo, Eleni was told to stay hidden from all Gutars, as her father called Gotland's people.

And Eleni obeyed, but only because she had determined the ship was too far from shore for her to swim to freedom.

Pekka, Jakob, and Akseli rushed to load the new cargo aboard the *Saari*, because now they, too, had begun to fret about the long voyage that stretched before them through uncertain weather. Eleni's father announced they must make it across the great expanse of the much-feared Northern Sea, and down the Minch, the dangerous Scottish strait, and reach the west coast of England before the fiercest autumn storms began. He would sell his cargo in England, Eleni's father explained, and then they could count their coins as the *Saari* skimmed down to Spain, where Eleni was to live a sheltered and chaperoned life. And from then on, he would visit her when he could.

They would eat sweet orange fruit until the juice ran down their chins, he promised.

But before crossing the great Northern Sea, the ship first had to make its way across two straits known by the fearful men onboard as "the cat hole" and "the triangle": Kattegat and Skagerrak.

Secluded though she was in her father's cabin, Eleni could

sense the sailors' worry as the *Saari* approached these two straits. Their chatter ceased. But the ship seemed to slide easily into the Kattegat, a famously dangerous expanse of water.

Now the *Saari's* great sail was raised no more than halfway up its mast, so as to give Eleni's father greater control as he moved across the Kattegat's confusing waters. The agile ship skimmed between dangerous flats, and islands more barren than any Eleni had yet seen.

They paused at Skagen, as if to catch their breath. Skagen was a fishing port at the northernmost tip of the kingdom of Denmark, and though that place's yellow houses—clustered near the town's flat, exposed beaches—gladdened Eleni's heart, seeming to wear the warmth of summer upon their sunny walls, she was given no chance to escape the *Saari* and swim to shore.

After resting but one day at Skagen, the ship sailed northwest into the Skagerrak triangle, heading for Norway's southern land, the Sorlandet. This water was easy sailing in the summer, her father promised, and both the ship and her sailors could gather their strength for their journey across the Northern Sea, which was sure to be the most difficult part of their voyage. In these calm waters, Eleni spent hours reliving her former life, and in this way she kept her mind busy, and her heart still.

She was already forgetting what her mother had looked like, Eleni realized sadly. In fact, it was so painful to think of her mother at all, that she began to scold herself when her thoughts floated in that direction.

So instead, Eleni thought of Matias. She recalled his sweet smell: like fresh green leaves. Eleni sighed, closing her eyes.

She could almost see his straight back, and his strong legs, and his determined chin, and the way his gold-brown hair fell against his neck.

Above the hold, footsteps thudded as sailors scurried across the lengths of timber supporting the heavily tarred fabric meant to keep the *Saari*'s cargo dry. Sometimes the steps paused on the small wooden roof over her head, as if a sailor—Pekka, perhaps, or Akseli—was trying to listen for any sound she might make.

But now Eleni was silent, too.

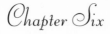

# Chapter Six

# Akseli's Turn

"I bought something for you, *tyttö*," Akseli said to Eleni the day after the *Saari* reached Mandal, the village at the southernmost part of the Norwegian coast. It was their last stop before heading across the great Northern Sea.

"We both did," Pekka called out, though Akseli ignored him.

The two young men had been allowed to go ashore that morning, but Eleni was bidden to stay onboard—with Jakob left behind to watch over her. It was as though her father now sensed something of Eleni's secret resolve to leave the *Saari*.

Akseli showed Eleni two small square baskets. A few strands of his greasy black hair flopped onto his forehead, partially hiding his round dark eyes. Several years older and half a head taller than Pekka, Akseli was night to Pekka's day, Eleni thought suddenly. Even Akseli's everyday mood was darker than Pekka's buoyant, sunny outlook.

One of the baskets Akseli offered was filled with new peas, nestled snug in their tender pods. The other basket was heaped high with tiny strawberries, fresh from someone's sheltered kitchen garden.

"But *I* bought you the strawberries," Pekka objected hotly. He tried to reach for the basket of berries, but Akseli blocked him with the turn of one bony shoulder.

"Do you want them?" Akseli asked Eleni, shaking the baskets a little as if tempting a puppy with a table scrap.

Jakob—busy mending the *Saari*'s spare sail—grunted to show his displeasure at this foolish competition. He looked around for Eleni's father, but Isä was still ashore. The ship's tarry casks of water had to be filled anew for the coming leg of their voyage, and more salted fish and hardtack bread needed to be bought and stored in barrels, to replace the food they'd eaten thus far. And new cargo was also to be loaded onto the ship, because the heavier they were, Eleni's father explained, the safer their voyage across the Northern Sea would be.

It had been many days since Eleni had eaten any fresh food, and she could not help but eye the peas and berries hungrily. "Thank you, Akseli," she murmured, finally accepting the gifts. "Thank you, Pekka," she called out, for it was difficult for her to see the boy, hidden as he was by Akseli's looming frame.

Eleni longed now for nothing more than to go below to savor her treasures in private, away from Mandal's unceasing wind, away from Jakob's disapproval, away from Pekka's growing frustration—and, most of all, away from gangling, bony Akseli, who had settled down next to her as if he meant to stay there for some time. He smelled sour, and Eleni wrinkled her small, sunburned nose.

"Pekka, come help me over here," Jakob commanded the younger boy. "It is Akseli's turn," he added half beneath his breath, and then he laughed as if at some private joke.

"Yes. Leave us, Squirrel Boy," Akseli called over his shoulder, not even bothering to turn all the way around as he delivered the insult.

Eleni bent her head over the two baskets. "Eat, *tyttö*," Akseli said, looking at her intently. He picked up a pea pod, split it with his grimy thumbnail, and turned its edges back, displaying the little peas inside. "Here," he said, holding it out as if Eleni might eat the peas from his hand.

"I can do it myself, thank you, Akseli," Eleni told him, flustered. "You eat that."

Akseli frowned, but he scraped the podful of peas into his mouth.

And although Eleni did not know why she did it, she started in on Pekka's berries, rather than Akseli's peas.

"You should not tease me so," Akseli said, scowling now.

"I do not mean to tease," Eleni said, surprised that he would say such a thing.

And it was true; Eleni had certainly not meant to anger Akseli. But she craved sweet things and would always eat them first, given the chance. She closed her eyes as she tasted the fruit. "Mmm. But I am grateful for the peas, too, Akseli." She opened her eyes and tried to smile at him.

"And now you laugh at me," Akseli said, clasping his strong hands together so tightly that the bones showed white. "You talk kindly only to Pekka the dunce. *Squirrel Boy*," he shouted at Pekka, suddenly angry.

"You be quiet," Pekka cried. He started toward them, but Jakob pulled him back.

Eleni's heart was pounding now, but she was determined

Akseli not know how much he frightened her. "Pekka is not a dunce," she said, keeping her voice steady. "My father relies on him, in fact."

"But your father relies on me, too," Akseli told her. "He relies on me *more*."

"That's not true," Eleni replied. "Each person onboard has a job to do."

"Except you," Akseli muttered, angry now. He narrowed his eyes. "We started on this voyage late because of staying at Lågnäs those extra days, didn't we? While your mother was dying? And then we had to linger off Inkoo until your father could rescue you from the Swedes. As if we had all the time in the world!"

"But that could only have cost the *Saari* an extra day or two," Eleni objected. "Or three, at the most."

"A day or *three* can mean the difference between life and death when storms start rolling in from the north," Akseli said, curling his lip at her ignorance. "And with an extra person onboard, we run through our food and water that much faster. It's no wonder we have to keep stopping for new provisions. Delay after delay! And just look at this place." Akseli gestured dismissively toward the little village at the end of the pier.

In spite of the wind, it seemed like heaven on earth to Eleni. She would live here in Mandal forever, she told herself fiercely—if only she got the chance. "None of this is my fault, Akseli," she told the now-furious young man. "I don't eat much, and I can prove it. See?" she said, and she flung the strawberries and the peas over the side of the ship.

She had to bite her tongue to keep from crying out her remorse the second after she did it.

Jakob and Pekka looked up, but whether shocked at the sinful waste or at her unseemly display of emotion, Eleni could not tell. Her heart was pounding so hard now, she could hear neither the incessant wind nor the mewing of the gulls.

Akseli jumped to his feet. "That proves nothing," he cried. "What a stupid thing to have done!"

And Eleni knew he was right.

"That's a fine way to woo, Akseli," Jakob called out, laughing so hard now that tears streamed down his cheeks. "That's the way to woo her."

# Chapter Seven

# A Tragedy upon the Great Northern Sea

The *Saari* had well over three hundred miles of open water to cross on the Northern Sea before it passed between the Orkney Islands and the Shetland Islands at Scotland's northernmost tip. On the evening before their departure from Mandal, Eleni's father tried to show her this destination on the precious vellum map he kept scrolled in the cabin. But to Eleni, the Northern Sea on the map looked like a frightening empty void, and the pictured Scottish islands looked more like tiny splashes of milk on the stretch of kidskin than places where people might dwell. "Do folks really live on those spots of land?" she asked, feeling ignorant and shy.

Isä's laugh was rusty. "But the islands are quite big. You could get lost on almost any one of them, *tytär*," he said, using the loving name—*daughter*—that he had called her when she was a little girl.

"They look so small, Isä," she said doubtfully.

"You will learn better soon enough, as we sail among them," he said, rolling up the map, wrapping it securely in a supple length of leather and stowing it in his sea chest.

Eleni bit her lips together as she considered her reply, for she did not want to ruin this rare peaceful moment, or to anger her father.

So again, she was silent.

The steer-board creaked very early the next morning as the *Saari* eased away from Mandal. Eleni heard the heavy sail being raised, and she listened to the men call back and forth to one another. She now knew each of their voices well: Pekka's soft, rushed words, of course, and Akseli's snarl, which she now detested, and Jakob's grumble. And she knew her father's voice in her bones.

In the dim, dank cabin, Eleni strained to listen as the sounds from other ships surrounding them at Mandal faded away. Soon, even the frantic cries of hungry gulls disappeared, and Eleni felt herself encircled once more by the whispering sea.

Their first day out, the weather was fine as the *Saari* began to work its way in a northwesterly direction. The sea would be darker now, Eleni imagined, and the sky a much deeper blue. She patched a worn spot on the *Saari*'s second sail and mended a torn seam on one of Jakob's two shirts. The ship moved swiftly through the water, and that night, her father seemed pleased at the progress they were making.

Their second day out, it was as though the Northern Sea decided it was time to test the ship a little. The *Saari* toiled up and slid down steep crests of seawater, and Eleni's stomach churned.

That night, when they were alone together in their small, triangular cabin, Eleni's father cocked his head as though listening for something. He left Eleni at midnight to go above to help Pekka, Akseli, and Jakob keep watch—for what, Eleni could not guess.

Underneath its waterproof covering, even the new cargo the sailors had brought onboard at Mandal seemed to signal its unease as the hours passed, shifting as the *Saari* dipped and rose. The sailors cursed in the night, and one of them scrambled below to stow the barrels and crates more securely.

Alone in her tiny cabin, Eleni tried to remember how to pray—either to Jesus or to Ahti, the ancient god of the deepest sea, which was what this must surely be. She did not think it mattered which deity she prayed to, so she tried them both.

As the third day dawned, Eleni awoke to a sudden urgency in the men's voices, and a stillness in the air told her something was about to change.

And then thunder crashed, and the side of the *Saari* was hit by the first massive wave churned to life by a storm she could not see. Eleni was thrown across the cabin by the wave's impact, and she slammed so hard against a sharp corner of her father's sea chest that it gashed open the upper part of her arm. Horrified, she stared at the gaping wound, fearing she might not be able to hold its startled edges together. Mercifully, the wound did not yet hurt, so great was her shock.

Would her flesh have to be pucker-sewn shut with crude black stitches by the rusted needle she used to mend the sails? Eleni did not want any of the men—even her own father!—to touch her tender flesh with his rough hands.

Not that there was any time for that.

The storm quickly became so savage that Eleni was unable

to stand, so she crawled back onto the sail that made up her bed. She tried to staunch the flow of blood as best she could with her kerchief, now wrenched from her head and wrapped tight around her arm.

And in the center part of the boat, the newest cargo came loose from its ropes once more.

Eleni felt the *Saari* turn then, to point into the wind. She knew this would gain Pekka and Akseli a few moments' time in the hold, to secure the now-dangerous cargo. Above her head, she heard her father and Jakob struggle to lower the big sail to half its former height, for the same expanse of sail that enabled the ship to skim along the water on fine days could be the very thing that might sink them in foul weather.

The sail might then become their shroud.

The ship resumed a more cautious course then, toiling up the side of one wave and sliding down into the trough that waited on the other side. Eleni shivered on her makeshift bed, and she bit her lip as her arm began to throb. She began to imagine they all were being devoured by this new creature the Northern Sea had become. Might they be eaten in giant up-and-down bites they had no hope of escaping? The noise of the storm was unceasing and terrible, and the groaning *Saari* sounded as though it might break apart at any moment.

Her father and Jakob—still working above—might have tied themselves to the mast by now, Eleni thought, though they had to control both sail and steer-board. Pekka and Akseli, working below, would be trying to stow cargo yet again as they also bailed water.

And Pekka was shouting out his prayers.

Seawater sluiced into Eleni's little cabin now, but she could do nothing about it, for heavy cargo had crashed against her cabin door, almost splintering it.

Someone was going to die this day. Eleni knew it.

Perhaps it would be all five of them!

It would be a tragedy upon the great Northern Sea, only one of many that had happened throughout the ages. And Matias would never know what had become of her. Would he even wonder?

An unidentifiable shriek from the cargo area returned Eleni to her senses, and she crawled through an inch or two of sloshing, icy seawater to the cabin door so she might hear what was happening. Frantic, she wrenched at the cabin door—which opened, to her immense surprise, for the cargo pinning it shut had shifted away once more.

"It's his arm," Akseli was shouting to the two men above. "Hold steady, Pekka—while I move this barrel."

Another horrible cry sliced through the din of the storm. "Äiti!" Pekka howled, calling for his mother.

"It's crushed," Akseli called out to Eleni's father, but his words disappeared, swallowed by another crack of thunder.

"Then tie it to his side," Eleni's father shouted down from above. "Pekka can use his other arm to bail. We need every man if we are to survive!"

"No, no, don't touch it," Pekka begged as the *Saari* began to force its way almost straight up the slope of another, bigger wave, and Akseli tried to secure what was left of the boy's arm.

"Bail water with your good hand, Pekka," Eleni heard Akseli scream angrily. "Bail, dunce, or you'll be the ruin of us all!"

"No, wait," Eleni cried.

Akseli turned to stare at Eleni in the doorway just as the *Saari* neared the top of the greatest wave yet. Her hair sprang from her head in pale, tangled masses, blood streamed down her wounded arm, and her skirt clung to her shaking legs.

Akseli seemed to be more afraid of her for that moment than he was of the storm.

And then the *Saari* slid down the far side of the giant wave, and more barrels flew through the air. Pekka shrieked again as he fell against some tumbling casks.

Clinging to the cabin door, Eleni gaped at the appalling scene in front of her. The hand at the end of Pekka's shattered arm flopped back and forth like a small white fish. "I can bail water," she cried out, forgetting her own wounded arm. "Let me bail for Pekka!" And she stepped into the hold.

"You? Bail for *Pekka*?" Akseli shouted, newly enraged. He seemed suddenly to grow bigger before Eleni's startled eyes. "Then Pekka goes above, girl, if you are able to work below," he cried out.

And Akseli grabbed the sobbing, begging boy and forced him up through the flap that opened to the makeshift deck above, and into the mouth of the storm.

Pekka could not grab hold of any man's hand or cling to any rope, of course, and so one final hungry wave was all it took for the fair-haired boy from the north to disappear over the side of the *Saari*—to be swallowed forever by the great Northern Sea.

# Chapter Eight

# An Evil Promise

The *Saari* sheltered at Kirkwall, in a snug bay on the biggest of the Orkney Islands at the very north of Scotland. The little ship tied up toward the end of the town's shorter pier. Two crates of linen and a huge pile of kelp soon sat nearby, waiting to be loaded aboard.

"It was because of you," Akseli muttered to Eleni as he and Jakob made room for the new cargo while Eleni tried to stay out of their way. Jakob was busy with his task some distance from them, and Eleni's father was pacing Kirkwall's narrow streets. He grieved for Pekka, who had been like a son to him, Eleni realized now. Eleni held her injured arm to her side, trying not to move it. It felt heavy now, and the wound was hot, its edges raw and puffy. A fever was beginning to spread throughout her shivering body. But she tried to hide this, because what did one small injury matter compared to what had happened to poor Pekka?

She could almost see his broken body hanging suspended in the cold dark sea—like a Lågnäs scarecrow in a midnight field, Eleni thought, shivering again.

"If you had stayed in the cabin," Akseli continued, "I would not have grown as angry as I did, and Pekka would still be alive. You bring bad luck upon us all."

"I do no such thing," Eleni answered, taking care to keep her voice as low as Akseli's. She did not want to alarm Jakob— or add to her father's misery, for Jakob was sure to relate any shipboard quarrel to him at once. "I do not even want to be on this ship, Akseli," Eleni continued. "You should tell my father what *really* happened, and not keep saying that Pekka lost all reason and climbed through the tarp and into the storm, and that was why he died. It is a lie, and you know it, too."

"It is *near* what happened," Akseli said sullenly.

"'He who lies three times believes that he has told the truth,' is that it, Akseli?" Eleni said, quoting one of her mother's sayings. She refused to deny the *real* truth of what had happened to Pekka. She could honor his death in that way, at least!

"Do not try those old words out on me," Akseli said. "What I told your father *is* the truth. I have decided."

"Oh, yes," Eleni said, mocking him. "It's all true, except for the part where you pushed a helpless, screaming boy into the mouth of a deadly storm."

"Because of *you*," Akseli was quick to answer. "And do not try to turn your father against me by telling him your crazed story, *tyttö*."

*Girl.* That had been Pekka's name for her! "It is the truth, Akseli—and do not call me by that name," Eleni told him. "I am my father's daughter, and you must respect me as you respect him."

"But you used to let *him* call you that," Akseli said, speaking of Pekka. His face twisted with remembered jealousy and fresh anger.

"Pekka was a boy who missed his family, and we were friends," Eleni said, realizing as she spoke that it was true. Pekka *had* been a friend to her—and she to him, she hoped.

Pekka, so cheerful about a hard life that he never chose for himself.

Pekka, who believed in luck.

"Anyway," Akseli said, turning away from her, "your father will not listen, even if you tell him. He needs me onboard more than he needs you, especially now that we are one man short. If you could have called Pekka a man."

"My father will try to find someone else in Kirkwall," Eleni said. "Perhaps that is what he is doing right now," she added, looking toward the busy little town. Surely there would be someone in this place who would join the ship!

As if any decent sailor would be willing to come aboard the poor tattered *Saari*, limping its way toward Spain, Eleni thought, contradicting herself at once. Rumors of the ship's bad luck—and the girl onboard—had probably already spread throughout the town.

"If he can rouse himself to do it," Akseli said, laughing a little. "Perhaps *I* will have to take over this ship, and soon," he added, tilting his head in a considering way. He flashed a quick glance in Eleni's direction, and he grinned. "When I do, *tyttö*, you will answer only to me. And that is my promise."

And an evil promise it was! Eleni could not hide her shivers now, and Akseli laughed when he saw the gooseflesh on her thin, exposed wrists.

Isä would *not* find another sailor in Kirkwall, Eleni knew suddenly. Might her father put Akseli ashore, if he knew what had really happened to Pekka? Perhaps. But then what would happen to those remaining aboard the *Saari*? Her stubborn father would make sure the ship continued to make its way south, Eleni knew, and that voyage might well be doomed without Akseli onboard to do his share of the work.

No. Her father could not risk losing another of his sailors, not with the perils of the Minch awaiting them. This passage through the Inner and Outer Hebrides—the western isles of Scotland, Eleni remembered—was renowned for its danger, but any attempt instead to sail way out into the Atlantic Ocean to the west of the Outer Hebrides would cost them days and days of valuable time, and likely prove to be even more dangerous.

So the Minch it had to be.

She would tell her father the truth about Pekka and Akseli when they reached Spain, Eleni decided. He would be stronger then, and better able to hear what had happened. And then he could punish Akseli as he saw fit.

Until that day, in spite of how much her father blamed her for Pekka's death, he would protect her from Akseli—but only because she was his daughter, his *possession*, and his pride was at stake.

Not for any other reason, Eleni knew.

During the *Saari*'s brief stay in Kirkwall, Eleni spent a lot of time peering at her father's old vellum map, examining the inner passage they were to take. And what she saw there both confused and frightened her, especially the tiny image so carefully drawn in the narrow curve that made up the Minch. The drawing depicted a small blue man poking his head out of the water as he swam. His flowing whiskers streamed behind him like whitecaps, and his little cheeks were puffed.

"Who is this, Isä?" Eleni asked her father one night, touching the tiny figure with her fingertip.

But her scowling father swatted Eleni's hand away from the map. "You won't ask so many questions when we're sailing in the 'Stream of the Blue Men,' child—the *Sruth na Fear Gorm*. For that same creature you're pointing at will bring us down to the bottom of the Minch if he can. And believe me, he would like nothing better."

*Chapter Nine*

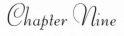

# In the Stream of the Blue Men

Eleni's father waited two more days, until the late-summer weather was fine, before sailing the *Saari* slowly past Kirkwall's old Brough Head lighthouse. He wanted to give his small ship every advantage in facing the Minch—and the frightening blue men who swam in its stream.

None onboard seemed to question their existence.

Just beyond the cabin wall, and through the veils of her now-growing fever, Eleni heard Jakob and Akseli talking in the hold, though they tried to keep their voices low so her brooding father would not hear. He was above, alone, Eleni knew; he had not even *tried* to find a Kirkwall man to sail with them.

"Maybe it's only because the seabed of the Minch is so tumbled and uneven," Jakob was saying only a few feet away. "Perhaps that's why the passage is so bad."

"There's far worse waiting for us out there than a bumpy seabed," Akseli scoffed, his usual rough voice now a worried rasp. "You know very well the water can drop, Jakob, and for no earthly reason. I heard of a galley that went nose-down to the depths of the Minch that way—and it was never seen again."

"You heard, you heard," Jakob jeered nervously.

"It was the blue men who made it happen," Akseli said, stating this as if it were a fact. "They hopped right onboard to bewitch its sailors, and no one could complete their tricky rhyme. *That's* why the galley went down."

"But the blue men don't even need to hop aboard," Jakob replied. "Because they can blow up a storm before you can say your prayers."

As if that might be a better way to die!

"So you'd better say your prayers now, old man," Akseli told him, laughing—although it sounded to Eleni as though he might start crying at any moment.

The *Saari* entered the North Minch on a fine day in late July, seeming to slide into its infamous stream as though the way had been greased for them.

This only made Isä's habitual frown more pronounced, however. "Easy *in* is not the same thing as easy *out*," he observed gloomily.

Eleni shared his dark foreboding, though the bad feeling she had about the coming stretch of their journey was blurred by her pain and her growing illness. She felt both ice and fire at the same time. Sweat poured off her feverish body, but she huddled under whatever covers she could drag over her while she shivered. Her wound throbbed all the time now, and faint red streaks were beginning to radiate from its strained edges as if reaching for the rest of her body.

This was a very bad sign, Eleni knew. But her father was so lost in his own misery that he never noticed a thing.

All the men were above. The *Saari* was about to enter Little Minch, the most dangerous part of the passageway through the Inner Hebrides, and every sharp eye was needed to make sure the ship made it through: past the rocks hidden just under the water's surface, their presence betrayed only by the restless thrashing of the water above; around any sudden whirlpool or hole the blue men might conjure up; between the foamy rips and bubbles that signified who-knows-what?

Eleni awoke with a start. When the men crept gingerly across the timbers above the hold, she could almost feel the sailors' footsteps in her bones. But now, no one walked above her head. Instead, the men clustered more toward the boat's fore, their sounding leads dangling, since that was where danger first would greet them.

At least two of the men would be lying belly-down, Eleni knew, and they'd be peering anxiously at the water as the *Saari* crept through Little Minch.

The softest and squelchiest thud that Eleni could imagine hit the outside of the ship just behind her head. It was quickly followed by another thud, even softer.

And Eleni knew she was no longer alone.

*"It's a lass,"* a strange voice whispered, sounding surprised, as the *Saari* continued to slip through the icy water of the Minch.

*"I know that,"* a second voice said, clearly annoyed. *"I can smell her lassiness, can't I?"*

Eleni's lips went numb. "Are you the blue men who live in this sea?" she finally whispered. "And are you Finnish, too?"

For she could understand their words, Eleni thought, surprised—and so they must be from her land! How strange that they would be dwelling here.

*"She says she's Finnish,"* the voice of the first blue man announced, ignoring her questions. *"We could use a girl to cook pulla for our clan. We must drag this ship to the bottom of the Minch, or we will lose her to the others. I will loosen its steer-board, and we can add it to our fine collection."*

*"The Swedes cook better than the Finns, in my opinion,"* the second blue man argued. *"And besides, this girl is ailing. She'll be ours soon enough when she dies and the sailors throw her over the side, don't you think? There's no need to go to all the bother of taking the ship. I'm too weary,"* he added, whining a little.

"And I cannot cook at all," Eleni whispered, thinking she must be honest with these—these *creatures*, whatever sort of beings they might be.

*"You'll have all eternity to learn,"* the first blue man said, laughing at her feeble protest.

*"Wait,"* the second one said. *"She can understand us!"*

*"Why, so she can,"* the first blue man agreed, startled. *"How is it you can speak to us, lass, and hear our words?"* he asked Eleni loudly.

"I do not know," Eleni answered, and that was no more than the truth.

The blue men conferred softly, their liquid whispers hidden by the silk-rustle rush of water as it slipped past the *Saari's* sides.

*"Are you a sprite, too, lassie?"* the first one asked, the dawning of mingled respect and concern in his burbling voice.

"I am not," Eleni admitted reluctantly. She was willing to claim any peculiar thing at all to save her life, but she knew there was no point in lying to beings so clearly supernatural.

She was a twilight child, but she was not a *sprite*.

There was silence for a few heart-stopping moments. *"She might not know it if she is a sprite,"* the second blue man finally said to the first. *"What is your clan?"* he asked, addressing the question to Eleni in the slow, patient voice people in Inkoo had used with Simo, the simple-minded man who swept the pier to earn his bread.

*"She's Finnish,"* the first blue man reminded his questioner. *"She has no clan, poor thing. At least not like the clans we have here, where things are civilized."*

*"Who are your people, then?"* the second blue man asked.

"My father is the captain of this ship," Eleni whispered, feeling weaker now than when the blue men had first started questioning her. She felt so weak, in fact, that she wanted nothing more than to slip into the stream of sleep that is the widest passage on this earth—and to disappear into it forever. She was very near to doing so, she knew.

*"And your mother?"* the insistent voice questioned.

"My mother is dead. But she was human, too," Eleni replied, feeling almost apologetic.

The blue men seemed to ponder this news sadly as they clung to the rear of the boat.

"My mother told me I was born at twilight," Eleni added, trying to add some words that might, after all, make these creatures think they had been correct. "She said that is an enchanted time of day. And it is true I met some beings in Finland whom others could not see."

"*She is a twilight child,*" both blue men said together, much pleased.

"That explains it," the first one said to the second. "*You were right!*"

"No, it was you who were right," the second blue man said, full of admiration for his fellow.

"We were both right," the first one gloated.

A satisfied silence seemed to seep through the *Saari*'s clinker boards. "Are you still there, sirs?" Eleni asked timidly, after a moment.

"We are," the first blue man confirmed, sounding absent-minded.

"*We are thinking of what to do with you,*" the second one said, explaining their silence. "*You are in danger on this ship, lass, even if we don't take it down with us right here and now. And there is no escaping that danger.*"

"Because of Akseli?" Eleni asked, her heart thudding once more.

"*Who is Akseli?*" the first blue man asked sternly—sounding more like a suspicious father than a creature of the sea.

"He is one of the sailors onboard," Eleni told him. "He has made it clear that he means to do me harm. And he killed poor Pekka, too."

"*Who is Pekka?*" the second blue man asked.

"He is the sailor who was swept overboard in the Northern Sea," Eleni whispered sadly. "Do you know him, sirs? For he dwells among you, now."

*"She has nice manners,"* the first blue man remarked.

*"He did not die in the Minch,"* the second one replied firmly, as if that were answer enough to Eleni's question.

Another silence.

*"We must not leave you in this peril, twilight child, even though we cannot tell you what it is,"* the first blue man said. *"You are too close to being one of us."*

"One of you?" Eleni asked, startled.

*"But we must slay the sailor Akseli,"* the second blue man said, clearly making this decision as he spoke.

*"Nothing easier,"* the first blue man said cheerfully. *"I'll go get him now, and we will drag him to the center of the earth until his stinking bubbles stop."*

"Oh, no," Eleni cried out in protest, for she knew suddenly she could not bear to be the cause—however indirectly—of another person's death. Even Akseli's.

She prayed she would not regret this decision.

*"Do you love him, then?"* the second blue man asked, sounding disgusted in advance.

"I do not!" Eleni exclaimed. "But even Akseli should live out his natural life, sirs, however long and wicked that life might be. Let me finish one of your tricky rhymes, if that will save him."

*"Our—our rhymes?"* the first blue man sputtered. *"Why are you human folk always so eager to spew rhymes at us, even as you drown?"*

"But that is the lore," Eleni explained, confused. "Do you not know the lore?"

*"The lore,"* the second blue man sneered. *"As if bad poetry ever saved anyone!"*

*"We have our own poets, lass,"* the first blue man said, obviously trying to be courteous to Eleni.

*"Anyway, that is not what matters,"* the second blue man reminded the first, although he still sounded a little disappointed that Eleni had asked them to spare Akseli. *"Remember?"*

They conferred again in inaudible whispers.

*"You must leave this ship in Tobermory, lass,"* the first blue man finally said. *"For kind people live there, and they will heal all that ails you."*

*"Promise,"* the second one told her. *"Or we will take the* Saari *down now, so you may dwell with us forever in the beautiful Minch. You needn't cook,"* he added kindly.

"I promise," Eleni whispered hastily. "I will leave the ship in Tobermory, if we stop there."

*"You will stop there,"* the second blue man said.

*"And remember always to be kind to selkies, for they, as well as we, are your honorary kin,"* the first blue man said, his voice growing fainter.

"I promise," Eleni said again. "But what are selkies, please?"

*"Seals, girl. Though they sometimes work magic and walk among men."*

*"And be kind to puffins,"* the second blue man continued, his voice faint. *"And to all other creatures who dwell on or in the deep. They may rely on you to care for them,"* the mere idea of a voice drifted in to her.

"I promise," Eleni told the blue men for the third time, as they slipped back into the Minch without a sound. "And thank you. And good-bye!"

Eleni's father celebrated making it through the "Stream of the

Blue Men" for the fifth summer running by doling out double portions of grog to his two remaining men.

"And there's more of that waiting for you in Mallaig," he promised, laughing, as the *Saari* ducked west through the shelter of Cuillin Sound and headed for the little port on the Scottish mainland. But as they rounded the Point of Sleat and were just off the southernmost tip of the Isle of Skye, about to make the final run east to Mallaig and its pleasures, a cold wind began suddenly to blow from the north, surprising everyone but Eleni, who suspected the blue men's handiwork. The wind swooped down the Minch, skidded straight over the Isle of Skye, and caught the *Saari*'s sail hard, knocking the ship off course and sending it south.

Jakob groaned as he tried to control the steer-board, and Akseli struggled to set things right with the sail, but the ship was now heading southwest. There was nothing to be done but to follow the wind's bidding. "We'll aim for the island of Eigg," Eleni heard her father shout. "We can shelter there for the night."

*Eigg*, Eleni thought dully in the triangular cabin below. She hoped Tobermory was there, so she could do as the blue men had said and leave the ship behind. Once in Tobermory's harbor, Eleni vowed, she would sneak above while the men were dizzy with grog, and plunge into the bay and hope for the best, because she knew she was now far too weak to swim. Perhaps an enchanted seal would save her.

But the strong, cold wind skidded the *Saari* right past Eigg's stony shores, and it was all Jakob and Akseli could do to control the steer-board and sail.

As the *Saari* rounded Ardnamurchan Point, the outermost

tip of a great lump of mainland poking into the Sea of the Hebrides, the wind suddenly failed. The *Saari*'s dark sail began to flap uselessly, and Eleni's father grew so angry with this bad luck that he ordered it hauled down and stowed. "Get out the long oars, men," he said as the ship drifted slowly past a knobbly point, toward the Sound of Mull. "We'll head for Tobermory Bay, instead."

Tobermory!

"Thank you," Eleni whispered to herself—and to whoever else might be listening.

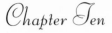

# Chapter Ten

# Over the Side

The *Saari* toiled into Tobermory Bay. The ship dropped anchor apart from the harbor's other craft, as if wanting to keep its distance. And then the weather began to change for the worse once more. If Eleni's father noticed the suddenly screaming birds, the heavy air, or the green and lowering sky, he said nothing to his men. But it was possible he was not aware of any of these omens, so relieved was he at having made it through the Minch once more—and befuddled as he was by both grief and grog.

Below, Eleni waited aboard the *Saari* for her chance to escape, not knowing how she would find the strength to take it if it came. Her arm festered, and her fever burned.

The door to the cabin gave a sudden rattle, and Eleni shrank back against the crumpled sail that was her bed. She feared it might be Akseli at the flimsy door, wanting to torment her while her father was in his drunken state. But it was her father himself. "We'll row ashore now, *tytär*," he mumbled, poking his shaggy head into the small room. "I'm leaving you onboard, though. A public house is no place for a captain's daughter."

A captain's daughter! So that's what she was now, Eleni thought dully, trembling in the gloom. But she was glad her father was leaving her behind. Her escape would be far easier once the *Saari*'s men were ashore.

"And don't try calling out to anyone, either," Eleni's father warned, seeming almost able to read her thoughts. "They'll be gabbling only Erse in these parts," he said, using what Eleni had learned was their word for the Gaelic tongue. "And folks won't know what to make of your words, should you start to squawk. Besides, as I told you, your home is on this ship until I deliver you to my lady friend in Spain."

"I know, Isä," Eleni said, since he seemed to be waiting for her reply.

Her father frowned, blinking into the gloom of their cabin. "You'll be much safer if I leave you here, *tytär*," he finally said with what almost sounded like tenderness. "If we *all* of us go ashore, that is," he added to himself.

Eleni thought suddenly that he might be thinking of Akseli as he spoke these words. "Yes, Isä," she said, closing her eyes. "Thank you. And good-bye."

The *Saari* rocked Eleni to sleep upon the bay's still-gentle swells, but when the small ship began pitching back and forth more forcefully, Eleni's eyelids flew open. How much time had passed? The ship was quiet, and Eleni felt confident its three men were still ashore. She even imagined she could hear their boisterous revels, although the wind was blowing so hard this was unlikely, Eleni told herself.

But the *Saari* was now swinging in such a wide arc, boards creaking, that Eleni grew concerned its anchor might not hold. If the line snapped and she were left drifting on this boat, what would she do? Could she rely on the blue men to save her?

Having no idea of when her father and his men would return, or even if the *Saari* was still anchored in Tobermory Bay, Eleni crept to the cabin door. She grabbed its handle and pulled herself as upright as she could, pausing briefly to glance back at the fetid cabin that had been her home for so many days.

She would not miss the *Saari,* she thought—if this were her farewell.

Eleni could see that the sailors had tidied the overcrowded hold while at port in Kirkwall, but next to a reeking pile of kelp she could still see the last place poor Pekka had stood, crushed arm flapping. Eleni said a prayer under her breath for his soul before she turned away. Then she crawled onto a barrel, turned aside a corner of the hold's waterproof covering, and stood clinging to the *Saari's* smooth wooden rail for balance, as the wind from the coming storm blew hard against her fragile body. She looked for the first time at the place where the blue men had told her she must live. It was as if she were a small seabird bobbing out on the waves, she thought, staring. Less than half a mile away, Tobermory seemed to reach out to her.

The small square buildings along the one-sided street facing Tobermory Bay glowed with color against the green of the hill rising so dramatically behind them, and the darkening sky only made those buildings look all the more magical to Eleni. Smoke from village chimneys both on the main street and from hidden hillside dwellings floated up white against the mingling darknesses of hill and sky.

A few small boats were drawn up on the smooth-packed stony shingle threading along the length of the bay, a dozen steps down from the street. Eleni thought she spotted the *Saari*'s small rowing boat, but she couldn't be certain.

Just to the left of the bay, a snub-nosed bluff jutted out, partially enclosing the ships that sheltered within the harbor. Eleni's eye was drawn to this place. There was a big stone house on the bluff, and its land was backed by a smaller wooded hill, and from some hidden place, a silver stream tumbled into the bay's choppy waters.

A small, white-aproned figure lurched unsteadily across a sloping stretch of close-cut grass as whoever-it-was hurried from one gray stone building—a fine barn?—to the house. It was a young girl, and she was being chased by a dark gray dog whose feints and prances only made the girl look all the clumsier. The solid-looking house's shining windows seemed to urge both dog and girl to hurry, hurry, because rain was starting to fall.

The girl stopped, however, and scanned the bay from the small bluff on which she stood. Eleni raised a timid hand in greeting. She did not know why she did this.

The dog barked—at her?—and the aproned figure seemed suddenly to lean forward, as though whoever-it-was had been startled to see movement on a ship that should have been emptied of its crew by now, with such a storm bearing down.

"Iona," a voice cried out from the big stone house.

The sound floated across the bay, and Eleni whispered the unfamiliar word to herself: "Eye-oh-nah."

The aproned figure hesitated one moment more, then turned away from the harbor and scurried toward the calling voice, bobbing up and down with the effort of moving so quickly across the lawn. The dog scooted after her, nipping at her heels as if he were herding her home. Eleni hated to see the little girl go.

Rain was falling harder now, and Eleni lifted her feverish face to the storm's insistent drops. She opened her mouth wide, as if to drink in the sky. Soon, she promised herself firmly, she would leap into the now-heaving water of Tobermory Bay and try to make her way to shore. Or she would drown.

Soon.

Her wounded arm hung hot and useless by her side, however, and in truth, Eleni did not see how she could find the strength even to hoist herself onto the *Saari*'s rail, much less to swim that half mile to shore.

But a sudden flash of light from one of the larger buildings on Tobermory's main street caught Eleni's eye, and she watched dumbstruck as a red front door opened just wide enough to let slip out some smoke, a few scraps of raucous laughter, and one tall, bony man. It was Akseli, and he was alone! Light shone dully on his lank black hair.

The man hunched down against the rain as if this might keep him dry, and he glanced back over his shoulder only once. Then he scurried across the road and down the stone stairs leading to the shingle, and to the little boats waiting below.

He was going to row out to the *Saari*.

There was only one reason for him to do this, Eleni knew, and with a single fluid movement, she was over the side.

Eleni plunged into the storm-black waters of Tobermory Bay like a white arrow. Golden bubbles of air streamed up from her body and disappeared. *Äiti,* she thought, wanting to cry aloud for her mother to come save her.

The water was so cold Eleni could feel little pain at first, other than a burning in her chest where precious breath longed to be replenished.

But she was becoming another creature now, she thought, surprised—one who did not hope for air to breathe, or for any comfort from this world.

Eleni began to struggle, however, because her body had a different idea.

And then a strong, storm-driven current swirled into the wide bay, and it pushed hard against her weakening body. She tried to cry out against this colder, bluer water, and a few last shining bubbles floated from her mouth toward the water's roiling surface.

And so Eleni followed them up.

# *Part 2*

# THE HEART
# OF THE WORLD

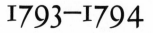

# 1793–1794

*"But when the wind failed, it was resolved
we should make for the sound of Mull,
and land in the harbour of Tobermorie."*

From "A Stormy Night at Sea" in
*"Boswell's Life of Johnson,"* Volume Five,
first published as *"A Tour to the Hebrides"*
1773

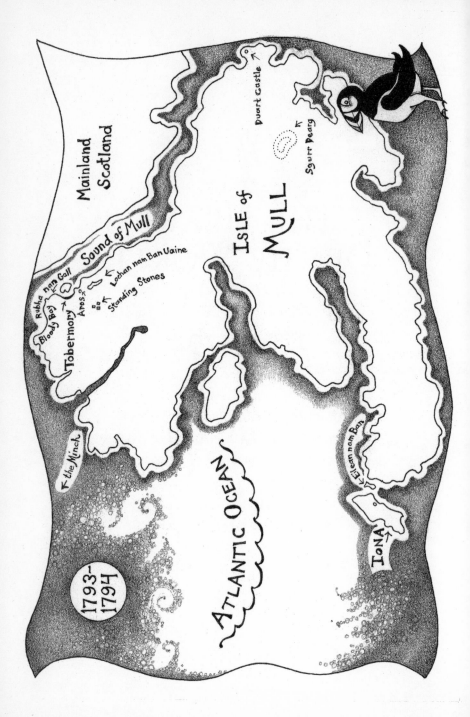

Mainland Scotland

Duart Castle

Sgurr Dearg

Isle of Mull

Sound of Mull

Rubha nam Gall

Lochan nam Ban Uaine

Bloody Bay

Aros

Standing Stones

Tobermory

the Minch

ATLANTIC OCEAN

Eilean nam Ban

IONA

1793-1794

# Chapter Eleven

# After the Storm

"The pirate ship is gone," Bethie—Aros's shorter laundry-maid—reported early the next morning, running into the big washhouse and slamming the door shut behind her to keep out the wind. "The one you told us about last night, Miss Iona."

Moira stopped work and leaned on her dolly peg, eyes sparkling, for this was exciting news.

"I never told you it was a *pirate* ship, Bethie," Iona objected. "And keep working, Moira," she added, speaking to the taller girl. "That sheet is not going to wash itself, and the storm has put us behind schedule." Moira went back to plunging and twisting the blunt ends of the peg in its tall wooden tub.

The laundrymaids looked at each other, however, and giggled at the little girl's bossy ways. Iona was only nine years old, but the older girls loved it when Miss Dundonald permitted her to join them in the laundry. The maids missed their numerous younger sisters, and Iona was a most satisfactory substitute.

The little girl was as sleek as an otter. In fact, she was so tidy in her person that Bethie and Moira joked secretly she was like a toy come to life. Iona's dark hair always gleamed like a chestnut. It was parted so exactly in the middle that it seemed Miss Dundonald might have used a length of yarn for guidance, the maids told each other, and it was pulled tightly to the sides into two narrow braids, with never a wisp of hair out of place. The braids hung over Iona's shoulders like shiny suspenders, giving her the air of a rich child's soldier doll. Even Iona's straight black eyebrows looked painted on, the laundry-maids marveled.

It was a pity about her fearsome limp, they agreed privately.

"Get to work, Bethie—we've wasted enough time," Iona scolded the second laundrymaid, but hearing herself, she began giggling, too.

"Tut-tut! We've wasted enough time," Moira said, saluting smartly as she marched around in a small circle.

"Don't tease," Iona said, pretending to be angry. "Just for that, *you* may use the punch today," she told Bethie, direct-ing the smaller girl toward the less strenuous task. But Moira didn't mind.

Iona smoothed her hands against her spotless apron as if she couldn't be bothered with such trivial things as naughty laundrymaids *or* vanished ships, but she made her way to one of the room's deep-set windows overlooking wind-whipped Tobermory Bay. She wanted to see for herself whether or not the strange-looking vessel was really gone. There had been a girl onboard, Iona remembered.

Or had she imagined that?

Guillemots and kittiwakes were streaming now across Tobermory's blue skies like endless black-and-gray ribbons,

Iona noticed, which meant they were returning to land, having flown out to sea just before the storm. "We must get those damp sheets back on the hedges, girls," she called out, turning around. "Shall I call for some help from the village?"

"No, dearie. We can manage," Moira told her fondly.

"I was right. The ship is gone, isn't it, Miss Iona?" Bethie called out, satisfied to have won her point. "Perhaps those pirates found the island's gold during the night!"

"Nobody has ever found the gold," Iona said, shaking her head.

"But the gold is real," Moira said solemnly. Two hundred years earlier, as everyone in these parts knew, brave Highland warriors had sunk the *Florida*, a galleon belonging to the fierce and deadly Spanish Armada, in Tobermory Bay. And ever since, rumors flourished throughout the entire island—and the whole of Scotland and England as well—of the 300,000 pounds worth of gold bullion said to have been aboard that ship.

"The pirates who were here last night might have tried to sneak ashore to steal *us* away," Bethie said, managing to look both frightened and thrilled. Her round cheeks flooded with pink.

Iona shook her head, as exasperated as an old maiden aunt at such silliness. "Pirates don't like chatterboxes," she told the maids. "And anyway," she added, "the ship I saw last night was just a rundown cargo vessel that had seen better days. Its sailors probably had too much to drink at the Gull, started a fight, and decided to take off while they could."

"You think those sailors left during the *storm*?" Moira asked, looking doubtful.

"Sometimes the open sea is the best place to be when the

weather's like that," Iona said, thinking of the birds, and of the seals that barked so noisily all around Mull's stony shores. They too went to sea when it stormed, Iona thought she had heard.

The laundrymaids nudged each other and laughed at Iona's pretended expertise. "That's the way to get to the *bottom* of the sea," Bethie told Iona.

"Let's get these sheets outside and on the hedges before Miss Dundonald calls me for lessons," Iona told the girls. "Or before she comes to scold." This made the laundrymaids hide delighted smiles, because Miss Dundonald was unlikely to scold even a mouse stealing her best Stilton, she was so generous and kind.

"Hurry," Iona cried, her hands on her hips. "Hurry!"

News about the *Saari*'s fate arrived with the late morning post.

"So it *is* at the bottom of the sea, Miss Iona," Bethie said toward noon, as she pumped water into the bucket that would fill her barrel. "Out at Rubha nan Gall, where the selkies like to gather. And it's true, because the news comes straight from Willie the Post. I saw him down by the lower hedges." She paused, smiled, and smoothed her hair back, remembering.

Moira and Iona exchanged startled glances, because none of the girls at Aros was supposed to be alone with any village man—especially not Willie the Post, who was widely known to toy with silly girls' affections. Only young Col Hardie had a worse reputation.

Miss Dundonald had her rules, meant mostly to guard her girls' honor.

"Willie said the ship was from Sweden or Norway," Bethie

continued, "or some such place, judging by the sailors' jabber he heard last night at the Gull & Gherkin. And Miss Dundonald knows about the wreck now, as well," she added, as if that settled things. "She saw the little boats from the village set out this morning to scavenge what they could, and when Willie came 'round with the letters, she grilled him good, he told me."

Iona almost felt sorry for Willie the Post, though he should not have talked to Bethie down by the hedge. He knew better.

"Willie told Miss Dundonald that its drunken sailors were chased out of the Gull & Gherkin at midnight," Bethie said, "just before the worst part of the storm hit. Only—their little rowing boat was gone! One sailor had already taken it, see, to go out to their ship. And so the rest of the men piled into poor Archie MacClellan's wee boat and rowed it on out. And then the foreign ship left the harbor, only to be dashed against the rocks out on the point. Archie is *that* angry to have lost his boat! But no one meant for the foreign sailors to leave the harbor, just the public house, they were so rowdy and wild." She paused, almost panting with excitement.

"Well, they didn't get very far," Moira observed with a snort, plunging and turning, plunging and turning her dolly peg. Her wiry light-brown hair sprang loose from its bun as her efforts increased, and it frizzed up like a halo around her long face.

And the ship *hadn't* gotten far, Iona thought—if indeed it had gone down where Bethie said—for the point was a small-ish lump on the far side of the great curved mass of land just northwest of Tobermory Bay. *"The nipple,"* rude sailors called this sticking-out bit, though the name really meant "strangers' point."

And "strangers" had always meant Norsemen in these parts, Iona recalled, struck by the neat coincidence of the ship from northern lands going down at this exact spot. "Are there any survivors?" she asked Bethie, thinking of the girl she was sure she had seen on that doomed ship.

"Survivors? None that I heerd of," Bethie reported, slipping into her old habits of speech for a moment. She spoke with what sounded like ghoulish satisfaction.

"They should . . . have . . . stayed . . . put," Moira said, twisting hard at her dolly peg.

*Plunge and turn. Plunge and turn.*

There had been a house on the bluff overlooking Tobermory Bay for as long as people could remember, and it was always called Aros. Built from rough gray stone, it had wooden trim painted sparkling white, and its shutters and door were glossy black. Gray, black, and white: the colors of the Dundonald tartan.

Everything about both the house and the washhouse was spotless, of course, both outside and in. Anyone who knew Margaret Maclean Dundonald would have expected nothing less, and that was what made her laundry such a success. She was so particular about its practices *and* its customers, that the fear of one's washing picking up other people's bodily pests or illnesses—a common concern elsewhere—simply did not exist here in Tobermory.

The lawns were always closely shorn at Aros, and the hedges

kept trimmed, and the enclosed kitchen garden—thoroughly dug by Margaret Dundonald and her mother themselves some thirty years earlier—was the house's secret treasure, full to bursting as it was with nourishing vegetables and sweet, juicy fruit.

Aros was set a little higher on the bluff than the washhouse. Miss Dundonald's mother made the old house fine after she'd moved there from Duart Castle in 1748, where she had been a Maclean. She died twenty years later, leaving her only child—a daughter, who'd determined never to wed—as the house's sole owner.

Now the house was home to Miss Dundonald, Iona, Bethie, Moira, Annie the housemaid, Pol the kitchenmaid, Mrs. Lochiel the cook, and Duddy the dog—Aros's only male, Miss Dundonald liked to joke.

In Aros's library, Miss Margaret Dundonald moved her wide, carved chair as close to the desk as she could manage, given her girth. She drummed surprisingly slender fingertips on the desk's gleaming top as she gazed out the window toward Tobermory Bay. Beside her, Duddy flopped down sideways onto a patch of window-paned sunlight that spread across the room's patterned carpet like melted butter, and instantly, he was asleep.

It was a terrible thing Willie the Post—that scoundrel!—had told about the lost ship, Miss Dundonald thought, brooding. The *Saari*, it had been called. And who knew how many souls were lost? Her tapping fingers itched to look the foreign word up in one of the room's many books, but she doubted she would find it, for no French or Gaelic words came close—except for the Gaelic *"sàr,"* which could mean either "excellent" or "hero," depending upon how you used it.

*"Saari,"* she whispered, trying out the word aloud.

Miss Dundonald sighed as she watched the bustle of activity along Tobermory's main street. Folks leaned into the wind as they cleared up after the storm, and scavengers would be making the most of things just around the great hump of land on the opposite side of the bay. It was a grisly but necessary occupation, Miss Dundonald reminded herself firmly.

She saw a tiny figure pause as it swept the shingle clean of its storm-tossed debris, and that person suddenly pointed toward Aros, her very own house. She could not hear the man call out, but he must have raised a cry, because others rushed across the street, pointed, too, and then clambered down the rough stone steps leading to the shingle.

Duddy lifted his head, listening. Then he held perfectly still.

The men started running along the shingle—and toward the sharp curve of the bay that led to Aros. They disappeared from Miss Dundonald's view just under her bluff, but she could hear their voices now, carried up toward her in scraps upon the wind.

"She's alive," one man cried.

Duddy began to bark—joyfully, Miss Dundonald observed, for she was the type of person who noticed such things.

And the dog dashed out of the library and into Aros's reception hall, where he waited with his tail wagging. *"Finally,"* he seemed to be saying. *"She's finally come!"*

# Chapter Twelve

## Poor Wee Lass

"It's a poor wee lass, miss," the first fisherman told Margaret Dundonald a few minutes later. He was wearing only a shirt and breeches, in spite of the chilly wind that was blowing outside, because he had used his heavy waterproof jacket to cover the near-naked girl as best he could. He held the unconscious Eleni out toward the woman as though he'd brought her a prize, and Duddy reared up, danced a minuet on his hind legs, and strained to get a look at the girl.

Behind Miss Dundonald, Mrs. Lochiel twisted her flour-dusted apron, and the housemaid, Annie, wrung her hands under her own apron, seeing Eleni's state of undress and the wild, unruly state of her flaxen hair. The maid reached up nervously to touch her own red hair, as if making sure it was still tidy.

"It's not a 'wee lass,' Miss Dundonald," a second man argued. "It's probably a wee *strumpet,* fallen drunk off the foreign ship that went down off Rubha nan Gall."

"But she couldna floated all this way around. Not this fast," a third fisherman pointed out.

"Then maybe the sailors threw her away before they left," the second man said stubbornly. "Her arm is all tore up, isn't it? Maybe they didn't want a broken strumpet aboard their ship."

"*Is* her arm all torn up?" Miss Dundonald asked, awakening from her stunned state. She reached forward to peek under the first fisherman's jacket. "Oh, dearie me," she said, horrified, seeing Eleni's sea-scoured injury. Duddy whined way back in his throat, and he danced around some more, seemingly trying to be of some service.

Miss Dundonald reached into her pocket-purse and jingled some coins. "Carry her upstairs, please, Angus—to the bedroom at the top of the stairs. Mrs. Lochiel and Annie, you go help Pol heat up water in the biggest kettle we have so we can clean the wound and bathe the poor child. Howie, you go fetch Dr. MacReady for me, would you? Quickly," she said to the third fisherman, who pocketed his coin, ducked his head in a respectful good-bye, and hurried off.

"And what about me?" the second fisherman complained, after Miss Dundonald drew the cords shut on her velvet purse.

"Don't be bigsy, Ian Mackay," Miss Dundonald said so softly that the man stepped back in fear, knowing instantly how angry she was with him. "You called her a strumpet! When this poor lass is better, you can tell her how sorry you are for having ever said such a thing. And then we'll see about your coin."

"Och," Ian complained—but softly, so that she would not scold him again.

"The girl's in a bad way, Meg," James MacReady said an hour later up in the small square bedroom meant for Aros's infrequent guests. "We'll have Mrs. Lochiel make up some horse chestnut tea for her fever, and maybe Pol can start pounding some comfrey for the poultice I'll slap on her arm after I bind up that wound."

"Oh, Jamie, just look at it!" Miss Dundonald said, appalled.

"She gashed her arm some days ago, it looks like," the doctor replied. "But the wound's well into the stage of digestion, Meg, and that's a very good sign. Shows it's trying to heal. I don't know why she didn't drown, but her time in the sea did something to help the cleansing along," he added, peering closely at Eleni's wound.

"Well, we should be glad of that, I suppose," Miss Dundonald said, sounding a little doubtful.

"You can help me finish washing it out, Meg, and then we'll dose it with some thyme oil to help stop the infection. The wound's past stitching, of course, but I'll close it up with some sticking plaster and bandages, and on goes the poultice, and then we'll hope for the best."

"Should I try to feed her something, Jamie?" Miss Dundonald asked.

"Tonight," he replied, nodding. "We'll start her on little sips of toast-and-water tea, then we'll move her up to pap in a day or two."

Margaret Dundonald nodded, biting her lower lip as she made the mental note.

"I know you'll do a fine job of mending her arm," she said. "Not a doctor in the world could have done better with poor old Duddy, when he got torn, and I'm sure you'll fix this girl up just as fine. Why, you sew better than a Belgian nun."

*

In the hall, Duddy wagged his tail, hearing his name spoken.

James MacReady hid his smile. "We'll keep that compliment about me sewing like a nun between the two of us, my dear, thank you very much," he said firmly. "Now, for her pain," he said, reaching for his bag.

"But she can't be having any pain," Miss Dundonald protested, looking at the seemingly unconscious girl. "Save the drops until she needs them, surely?"

"She'll need them in a moment, when I start paddling around inside her arm," Dr. MacReady said. "This poor girl is only pretending to sleep, Meg, and I'm not going to put her through any more trials than she has already endured."

"Do you mean that she can *hear* us, Jamie?" Miss Dundonald asked skeptically. She leaned closer to Eleni as if the girl might suddenly open her eyes and begin to speak.

"Aye, she can hear us," Dr. MacReady said. "Understanding us is something else, of course—for we don't know where she's from. But pain has no language, Meg. And so here we go," he said, measuring the precious drops of tincture of blue poppy that, mixed with a little water and spooned into Eleni's mouth, would sink the girl into the soundest of slumbers for an hour or two.

Outside in the upstairs hall, Duddy exchanged worried glances with a smaller being, then scratched frantically at the bedroom door.

An hour later, Miss Dundonald looked over her shoulder to make sure she and the doctor were truly alone, and then she leaned forward, taking care to keep her voice low. "The girl's very pretty, Jamie, in spite of all she's been through. How old is she, would you say? Two or three years older than Iona? Twelve, maybe?"

"Older than that," the doctor said, giving the neat bandage on Eleni's arm a farewell pat. "You can see how she's starting to bloom," he added delicately. "She's thirteen, or even a bit older, though she's small for her years."

"And—and is she a maiden still?" Miss Dundonald asked softly.

"Do you think I can determine that by looking at her *arm*?" Dr. MacReady asked, laughing. "You're not that daft, Meggie Dundonald!"

"I meant, as far as you can tell," Miss Dundonald said, blushing. "Not that it makes any difference to me, mind," she added hastily. "But I suppose we should know just how badly she's been treated, if we are best to help her."

"I'll wager this girl is untouched, Meg," Dr. MacReady said, "though maybe you'll be able to know better when you bathe and tend to her. She's been made ill by this nasty wound, of course, and she's bruised something fierce about her lower extremities. But time spent at sea on a beat-up old cargo ship will do that to a body. Why, I wish you could see under the clothes of some of the sailors I've treated!"

"No, thank you very *much*," Miss Dundonald replied primly, and Dr. MacReady laughed out loud.

"But once she mends," the doctor continued, "she'll ring as pure and true as a little silver bell."

Miss Dundonald sighed and shook her head, looking at the

girl. "Well, that's good news," she said. "And I'd appreciate it if you'd let her—her *purity* be known around town, Jamie, folks being as hard as they are on a new arrival to the island. 'Specially when she's pretty, and foreign, and she's fallen off a strange ship. Why, Ian Mackay was already flapping his gums about her."

"You know I never talk about my patients, Meg," the doctor protested.

"Oh, don't be silly," Miss Dundonald said. "Of course you do. So tell folks, please."

Dr. MacReady sighed and nodded his assent.

Miss Dundonald matched his sigh. "I suppose the girls and I had better bathe her now, before the blue poppy tincture wears away. But I don't know what I'm going to do about her hair," she said, looking at Eleni's hopelessly tangled locks. "Why, they're practically elf knots, I'd say."

"Elf knots?" Dr. MacReady asked, raising an inquiring brow.

Miss Dundonald laughed softly. "You know, Jamie—how the elves are said to snarl a person's hair up when that person is asleep so that they can use the knots for stirrups as they ride around during the night?"

"Oh, *elf knots*," the doctor said, as if all had been explained. "You wee witch."

"Jamie," Miss Dundonald scolded him, crossing herself. "You mustn't say that." She laughed a little. "No one would call me *wee*," she said, smoothing her hands over her belly, though in a satisfied way.

"You cut a fine figure, Meggie Dundonald," Dr. MacReady said admiringly. "But I do happen to have a potion for those locks, as it happens. Snip 'em all off while the girl is still asleep. It'll hurt her less that way, believe me."

"Cut off her *hair*?" Miss Dundonald echoed, as if she might have heard wrong.

"Well, what else would you do other than shear this poor wee lamb, Meg?" Dr. MacReady asked. "Hair grows back, remember. And she'll accept it better if she wakes up and the deed is already done."

"You're right, I suppose. It's just that it's—it's her *hair*. And it's not fitting to cut a girl's hair unless the moon is full."

"They're elf knots, Meggie. Get rid of 'em."

Eleni floated back into consciousness, but she didn't open her eyes. She tried to determine what was happening to her. It felt as though a large cat was licking her clean with a rough, flannelly tongue: under her arms, between her fingers, behind her bare neck. Was she dead, and being readied for the grave? Or could she still be under the sea, and being tidied by the blue men of the Minch? What an embarrassing thought!

Eleni didn't dare move.

"I think she's awake," Iona told Miss Dundonald, wringing clear hot water from another cloth and then handing it to the woman, who began work on Eleni's feet.

"Maybe so," Miss Dundonald said serenely. The girl *was* a maiden, she exulted; she'd swear to it in a court of law, were such a thing possible. Whatever else those poor dead sailors were, they hadn't been cowardly monsters who would molest a helpless young girl.

"Can she hear us, do you think?" Iona asked, longing to lift one of the girl's eyelids to see if she were really sleeping. "Maybe we should shout at her," she suggested, sounding hopeful.

"Don't you dare," Miss Dundonald told her. "We'll let *her* be the one to decide when she wants to talk to us—or learn to talk to us, if she doesn't yet have the Gaelic. And that is a thing that may take some time, my darling Iona, so we must be patient."

# Chapter Thirteen

# What Is Your Name?

Aros itself seemed to hold its breath as it adjusted to Eleni's presence, and upstairs, in what was now her bedroom, Eleni pretended to sleep. Really, though, she was listening to the chatter of an outlandish tongue. Although Eleni knew she was safe, the words swirling around her like water made her feel more alone than ever.

Sometimes, though, as she fingered the short, soft curls that were all that remained of her once-long hair, a friendly dog pushed his furry muzzle underneath one of her hands, and that was a thing that truly warmed her heart. *"Koira,"* she whispered, calling him "dog," since she didn't know his official name, and he could not tell her.

Duddy wagged his tail, and during those sweet moments, Eleni was glad to be dwelling in this strange place. She closed her eyes.

Dogs—like the sun, the moon, and the stars—were the same in every land.

It was some time later that Eleni opened her sleepy eyes once more. Had that small rustling noise been the wind blowing stronger over a choppy Tobermory Bay, as she now knew it sometimes did toward dawn?

No. It was not the wind, for the wind did not stop and start in just that way.

It was more like—like footsteps, Eleni thought, chilled. Not the tiny scrabbling step of a mouse, but not the purposeful tread of a person, either. This step belonged to some in-between creature. A twilight creature. *"Koira?"* she whispered, daring to hope for a moment that the loving dog had sensed the uneasiness the coming day had brought her, left the mat that was his bed, and was creeping into the room to comfort her.

There was a moment's silence. *"I am not Koira, who is really Duddy,"* a hoarse voice finally explained. *"Not that you could be expected to know that. I am a brounie—called Brounie. Hello."*

Eleni sat up so fast in bed that her pillow fell to the floor. Was she dreaming?

*"Now I'll have to dust that off,"* the voice said. The creature sounded aggrieved, but resigned.

"Brounie?" Eleni asked, trying to peer into the room's shadowy depths. "Are—are you the spirit who watches over this room?"

*"Well!"* the voice said, sounding a little offended. *"That is rather a quaint way of putting it. I would say I'm here by choice. It's just that I choose never to leave this house. It makes me nervous even to think about it, twilight child."*

"Who told you that's what I am called?" Eleni asked, her

heart thudding. "Was it Tonttu?" For this brounie creature—though she hadn't yet seen him—reminded her in some ways of the little *saunatonttu* she had loved, back in Inkoo.

*"I do not know anyone who is called Tonttu,"* Brounie told her. *"But then,"* he added, *"my social life is not all that it should be, what with me being kept as busy at Aros as I am—cleaning, and looking out for the selkie's child. And now there's you to look after, as well."* He sounded a little overwhelmed.

Confused and sleepy, Eleni tried to take in all that this small being was telling her. "Then who told you I am sometimes called twilight child?" she finally asked again. "And—and how is it we can understand one another's speech, Brounie, if you are Scottish and I am Finnish? And why are you speaking to me at all?"

The brounie sighed, as if bored by Eleni's questions. *"Who, and how, and why?"* he said, gently mocking her. *"Enough questions, child! I have come to greet you. It is simple good manners, at least where I come from. And the circumstances of your birth make you something of a kinswoman to me."*

The blue men had told her that kind people lived in Tobermory. But—honorary kin?

*"We will talk about it further some other time,"* Brounie said, seeming to read her thoughts. *"When you are stronger, child."*

"All right," Eleni said, blushing in the predawn gloom. "But tell me, Brounie, do the people living here know about you?" she asked, hoping the little creature had not left.

*"The big lady knows,"* Brounie said. *"I've even let her catch a glimpse of me, given her interests. But I've never spoken to her. It's important to keep some things in this life a mystery, don't you think?"*

"I—I hardly know what to think," Eleni replied. "Where do you come from, Brounie?" she asked after a moment. "And what is it exactly that you do in this fine house?"

*"I cannot tell you my origins, child, for that is a secret,"* Brounie said. *"But as to what I do here, why, I help with household chores left unfinished."*

"Do you mean that you creep out and—and dust the cobwebs away, and such?" Eleni asked, wishing that such a being had inhabited the Lady Sigrid's house in Inkoo.

*"I never creep,"* the brounie corrected her in a sharpish voice. *"I tiptoe quietly. I move silently. But only in the house. Pray, do not expect me to trim the hedges, twilight child."*

"My—my other name is Eleni," Eleni said shyly.

*"I have always known your names,"* the brounie boasted. *"Ever since you came here. 'Twilight child.' 'Eleni.' 'Lavendyre.' 'Eleni Lavendyre.' 'Ellen Lavender.' 'Ellen MacReady.' 'Äiti,'"* the brounie finished, sounding proud to have remembered them all.

Eleni's ears rang with these names—which seemed both strange and familiar to her at the same time. And "Äiti" sounded sweetest of them all, she thought, for it meant "Mother." But who would be her future baby's father, if not her childhood friend Matias? For there had been no mention of his name.

Where was he now?

*"We were not speaking of your friend,"* the brounie said sternly.

"But—how can you tell what I am thinking?" Eleni whispered, awed. "And how do you know these things?"

*"Again, I am not free to say,"* the brounie answered in a dignified voice. *"And I did not come here tonight to answer such questions."*

"The blue men of the Minch must have told you something about me," Eleni said, guessing. "Oh, Brounie, let me see you," she begged. For she was lonely, and she feared the creature might suddenly leave—just when she was beginning to know him.

*"I canna do that just now,"* the brounie said, sounding a little sad. *"But I can describe myself, twilight child. Would that please you some?"*

"It would," Eleni said, nodding in the gloom.

The brounie cleared his throat. *"Well, I'm wee,"* he began, as if confessing to some slight flaw. *"A bit shorter than Duddy, even. But I'm taller than an elf, and taller still than any fairy you ever saw."*

"Lots taller, I'll wager," Eleni said, backing him up.

*"Lots taller. Lots, lots, lots,"* the brounie agreed modestly, seeming pleased to use a new expression. *"And I'm as brown as a nut, of course, and my hair is a bit raggedy-like, but clean, mind you, and I like to sleep by the fire. And that's all I feel like telling you, child. Ask the big lady, if you want to know more. She can look me up in one of her books, though some of the details in them are wrong. As far as I'm concerned, at least. Some of the books even have illustrations, but I'm much more handsome than any badly drawn engraving, I assure you."*

"But I cannot understand her words, Brounie," Eleni said sadly. "Or the little girl's words, either, though she limps about and speaks to me almost without ceasing."

*"I think Iona is lonely, too,"* Brounie said. *"And no wonder! But just listen to her quietly, twilight child,"* the brounie advised, stifling a noisy yawn. *"Her words will begin to make sense before*

*long. Learning a new tongue is like trying to look at a tree's reflection in moving water. It is only when the water finally stills that the reflection becomes clear."*

Eleni shook her head, puzzled. "I do not understand what you are saying about the tree and the water, Brounie," she told him.

The brounie sighed. *"I suppose I overcomplicate things, child. And I am tired,"* he said, yawning once more.

"I'm not one bit tired," Eleni told him. "In fact, I don't think I have ever been more alert in my entire life!"

And yet she did not awaken until well after dawn.

"What language does the foreign girl speak, Miss Iona?" Bethie asked a few weeks later. She was working the punch again, while Moira was on the dolly peg.

"One of the northern ones, Dr. MacReady says," Iona replied. "She recognizes some of the Swedish the doctor tried out on her," she reported. "But she babbled on in another tongue as well, when her fever was at its worst." Iona paused, carefully sorting through finicky Mrs. Fraser's fine white laundry.

"But we already *knew* it had to be a northern tongue, Miss Iona," Moira said, continuing to plunge her peg up and down in its barrel. "That ship was from the north, the men all said," she added.

"She's a fairy, maybe," Bethie said, excited. "Perhaps she's been talking in a fairy tongue!"

"No," Moira scoffed. "Fairies are dangerous, as you well know, Bethie—and they're powerful creatures, too. Does that wee girl look powerful and dangerous to you?"

"No," Bethie admitted reluctantly.

It was a late summer day, beautiful and clear, and Moira and Bethie were hurrying to wash the sheets that had piled up during the past few rainy days. The girls knew they must take advantage of the sun for drying while the good weather lasted. Frequent plates of currant scones and shiny brown pots full of sweet tea brought from the kitchen by Pol fueled their efforts.

"It could be Russian she's speaking, Miss Dundonald tells me," Iona said thoughtfully.

"*Russian?*" Both laundrymaids were excited by this possibility. Although they considered Tobermory to be the heart of the world, attracting many foreign visitors to its harbor as it did, Russians were still a rarity.

"Well," Iona said, "Miss Dundonald and Dr. MacReady both say the girl *looks* a bit Russian, with her wide cheekbones and all. But it's hard to tell. She doesn't speak much, except to Duddy. I hear her whispering to him at night down the hall, when she thinks I'm asleep."

Moira shook her head in wonder at the thought of a grown girl talking to a dog—as if he were a Christian! But then, the idea of allowing a dog to live in a grand house such as Aros was so strange that perhaps talking to the friendly creature made its own kind of sense.

"I think she's beautiful," Bethie said with a sigh. "Her eyelashes are so long that they make shadows on her cheeks. But her shorn hair makes her look like a duckling."

"You'd look like a duckling if someone cut off all your locks," Iona said, gently scolding.

Bethie's eyes grew wide at the very thought.

"I think she's beautiful, too," Moira said shyly. "Her eyes are as green as willow leaves on a sunny day, and she trips along so light."

"I still say she's a fairy," Bethie whispered again, sighing happily. "Or—or maybe a Russian *princess*! She could have been kidnapped by those pirates. I'm glad they're all dead," she said, looking angry and fierce.

"Well, fairy or princess, the foreign girl will be able to come outside soon," Iona said. "Because Dr. MacReady thinks it will be good for her to get some fresh air and sunshine, and to be with other girls." *Besides me,* she thought, for the foreigner had not made the least attempt to speak with her yet, no matter how hard Iona tried to get her to talk. The girl simply curled up quietly on the far corner of her bed, turned her back, and pretended to be asleep.

Perhaps she did not want a Scottish friend, Iona thought mournfully. Or maybe it was Iona's limp that was making the new girl shy away. Perhaps the limp disgusted her!

"'The foreign girl,'" Bethie echoed. "We can't keep calling her that. I wonder what her real name is."

"That's a thing we'll probably never know," Iona said with a grown-up sigh as she carefully poured more lye water into the buck.

"Your name. What is your name?" Miss Dundonald asked patiently as she sat in her library with a frightened Eleni and an attentive Duddy, who kept looking from his mistress to Eleni, then back again. "Duddy," Miss Dundonald said, pointing to the dog. She enunciated the word clearly.

"Duddy" means "dog" in the big woman's tongue, Eleni told

herself, vowing to remember this important word. Forget *koira* forever, she added silently.

"Duddy," she repeated in her softest voice.

"Good girl! Good girl," Miss Dundonald enthused, and Duddy wagged his tail.

"Good girl," Eleni repeated obediently, though not knowing now what the big woman was talking about. But she ached to finish this lesson so she could go upstairs again, sit by the window, and wait for the *Saari*—and her father—to come for her. She did not want this to happen, Eleni admitted to herself, but she feared that it would. So she must prepare herself to leave this peaceful, happy place.

She must not allow herself to feel too much at home here.

"No, wait," Miss Dundonald said, waving her hands in the air.

"Wait," Eleni echoed, waving her own hands.

Miss Dundonald clamped her lips together so no more words could escape them. Then she had an idea. "Miss Dundonald," she said slowly, pointing a finger at the impressive swell of her chest.

Eleni stifled a gasp. "Misdundundun," she said, trying not to stammer as she pointed to her own, less impressive chest.

"Misdundundun" must mean "bosoms," Eleni thought, scandalized. What an odd word to teach her!

Miss Dundonald's face filled with disappointment, and even Duddy looked a little worried at Eleni's slowness to catch on. "Duddy," Eleni said hurriedly, pointing at the dog, for she wanted to make the big woman—and the dog!—happy again.

"That's right, dearie," Miss Dundonald whispered, praying

that Eleni would not repeat these words back to her. She took a deep breath, and then quickly, pointing as she spoke, said, "Duddy. Miss Dundonald. And—" and then she pointed at Eleni.

Eleni blushed furiously and pointed to her own chest once more. "Misdundundun," she said, miserable. Would this lesson never end?

Miss Dundonald threw up her hands in despair. "Well, I give up," she said aloud, but to herself. "For now, anyway. I thought I could manage to find out your name, but—"

Eleni bit her lips together and tried not to cry.

"Well, we're going to have to call you *something*," Miss Dundonald said after a few frustrated moments. The woman—looking rather like a small craft in Inkoo harbor, Eleni thought admiringly—got up from her desk and glided over to her tallest bookcase. She was much more graceful than the Lady Sigrid had *ever* been.

Eleni watched as the big woman pulled a book from the case, opened it with care, searching for the correct page, and then drew her index finger down the page until she found exactly the word she was looking for. She looked over at Eleni and smiled. "'Lavendyre,' that's what we'll call you," she said triumphantly. "Say 'Laven-deer,' darling."

Duddy wagged his tail some more, but Eleni was silent.

"Lavendyre," Miss Dundonald repeated. "That's the word they used three hundred years ago for a girl who worked in a laundry. It's from the Old French word *'lavandiere,'* lambie. You won't be working much in the laundry, mind, but you do live at Aros now. Perhaps folks in Tobermory will think of our washhouse when they hear your new name." She nodded decisively, and Eleni nodded back, wanting to please her.

"And since it's such a fine old word, we'll spell it the old way," Miss Dundonald announced.

Eleni tried desperately to guess what the big woman was trying to tell her.

"And lavender is a beautiful flower, too," Miss Dundonald said encouragingly, as if this might convince the baffled girl to accept her new name more readily.

"Duddy," Eleni whispered, and the friendly animal rushed to her side.

The dog had one brown eye and one blue eye, Eleni marveled—as if he'd been enchanted by one of the blue men, perhaps, and was here to comfort her.

"Well, it doesn't matter if you understand the word or not," Miss Dundonald finally said, some of the old Maclean impatience peeping through. "It's your new name, so you'd better learn it. 'Lavendyre.' Say it," she commanded.

"Laven-deer," Eleni repeated, not knowing where to point.

# Chapter Fourteen

# Sisu

Three months passed. It was the end of October, and Eleni was now able to tell the people at Aros her name. Hearing it, Miss Dundonald had grudgingly taken to calling her Eleni Lavendyre. The girls at Aros simply called her Eleni, however.

If it was a rainy day, which it often was on Mull in the autumn, Eleni and Iona finished their lessons as quickly as they could and made themselves comfortable in front of the fire in Miss Dundonald's library. There they read, drew, or embroidered wildflowers on pillowslips while Iona helped Eleni practice the two new languages Miss Dundonald had been teaching her, Gaelic and English.

Mrs. Lochiel, Annie, and Pol could always be counted upon to come up with a glorious tea on rainy nights. It was a relaxed late-night feast that everyone in the household enjoyed around the big kitchen table: savory little sandwiches, ginger-studded scones—candied ginger being a rare and special treat—and small sweet cakes.

If it was a day when Iona's lame leg hurt her, but the weather was too fine to stay indoors, Eleni and Iona were allowed to borrow Miss Dundonald's cart for short expeditions away from Tobermory, with Duddy substituting for Miss Dundonald as the girls' devoted guardian. This privilege was a recent thing, but Miss Dundonald had quickly come to trust Eleni's innate good sense. "If you're going to go all scatty on me, we might as well get it over with now," the woman declared, laughing. She knew that her Eleni Lavendyre would never let little Iona come to any harm. And the other way around, as well.

The gaily painted cart—pulled by Fancy, the prettiest and strongest Shetland pony on the island—was used mostly for delivering laundry, with the girls walking alongside, but it also provided a place for Iona to rest when her lame leg pained her.

One unexpectedly mild Saturday afternoon, the two girls and Duddy took the cart to visit the standing stones southwest of town. Soft ferns seemed to foam around the stones' bases like the green swells in Inkoo's harbor, Eleni thought, trying to remember every detail of that once-so-familiar place.

*Äiti,* she thought suddenly. *Isä.*

"Why are you sad, Eleni?" Iona asked, running her small hands lightly over the mossy surface of one of the ancient stones.

Eleni sighed. "I am not sad," she told Iona. "I only missing my mother and father little bit. Missing my home. Father, he drown in water. Out on point," she confided, gesturing in a westerly direction.

"Your father was on that ship?" Iona asked, flabbergasted. "The one that went down off Rubha nan Gall?"

Eleni nodded, solemn. She had learned the fate of the *Saari* weeks earlier, and only slowly, as she became better able to understand the words she was hearing in Aros's kitchen. Mrs. Lochiel had gone to the sailors' funeral with Miss Dundonald, and she was so moved by the three plain, unmarked coffins that she couldn't stop talking about them. "No names at all. Just like they was nobody's child," the cook kept saying.

Eleni knew, however, that her father would want just such a grave.

"But—but why didn't you tell us your father was on that ship?" Iona asked. "We thought maybe those men who drowned were pirates who had kidnapped you!"

"Kit-nap?" Eleni said, looking puzzled.

"Stole you away," Iona said, trying to explain. She piled a bunch of fallen leaves together, and then tiptoed her fingers up to the pile and snatched one, hiding it behind her back.

"Oh, yes, he stole me away from *Fru*," Eleni said, thinking that she understood the child's meaning. Eleni spoke cheerfully enough, but she looked a little sad.

"Poor Eleni," Iona said, her brown eyes looking tragic. "Was *Fru* your mother?"

"No," Eleni said, shaking her head. "She own me."

"She *owned* you?" Iona said, shocked. "Do you mean that you were a slave, Eleni?" Eleni looked confused. "Like—like we own Duddy," Iona said, trying to explain.

Eleni laughed. "Duddy a dog, Iona. He sleep all day," she said. "Me, I must work at *Fru*'s house all the time."

"But—you could leave her house whenever you liked, couldn't you?" Iona asked.

"Oh, no," Eleni told her, remembering. "I leave, *Fru* hit me one day! But then she is sorry."

"She *beat* you?" Iona said, her brown eyes filling with tears.

"Do not," Eleni said, reaching over to wipe Iona's cheeks dry. "No, Iona. Is good, now, for I am with you and Miss Dundun. And Duddy."

"All right," Iona said with a sniffle. "I'll stop crying. But I think you are a very brave girl, Eleni."

Eleni bit her lips together, for she did not wish to say anything—however accidentally—that might make little Iona cry again.

"Brave," Iona repeated, clenching her fists and shaking them in the air.

"Oh. *Sisu,*" Eleni said, pleased.

"'See-sue,'" Iona echoed.

"You, as well, Iona," Eleni said shyly, thinking of the little girl's painful leg, and how she never complained. "You, too, *sisu.*"

"Thank you, Eleni," Iona said, smiling.

"*Kiitos,*" Eleni told Iona, thanking her in Finnish.

"'Key-toes,'" Iona repeated, smiling. She looked down. "I don't miss *my* father," she said softly. "Or my mother, either—because I never knew them. I was a foundling, Eleni. That's what they call you when your mother and father run away and leave you behind when you are just a baby, and someone finds you."

Understanding many of Iona's words, Eleni was full of questions, but courtesy—and the limitations of her speech—made them difficult to ask. "In Tobermory?" she finally said.

Iona shook her head so slightly that her shiny dark braids barely moved. "No. It was on Iona, the holy isle just to the west of Mull, at the bottom of the island."

Eleni frowned, thinking hard. "What does 'holy' mean?" she asked.

"'Holy' means that the isle of Iona is a sacred place," Iona said. "Like a church, but even better than that. I was left swaddled in a sealskin, in the ruins of the abbey there, where the monks used to live in the old time. So I was named for the holy isle."

There were now so many unfamiliar words for Eleni to deal with that she had all but given up on the details of Iona's story. She understood her friend's sadness, however.

"None of the few people who live on the little isle knew anything about me, or so they claimed," Iona said, sighing. But obviously someone, perhaps a visitor to the island, decided to give birth to me there, or to throw me away." She picked up a handful of leaves, demonstrating, and let them fall to the ground.

"Not throw away, Iona. Not throw away," Eleni said, reaching out to touch Iona's small, cold hand.

Iona shrugged. "*Maybe* throw away, Eleni. Because I was injured, see. Dr. MacReady said my little bones were probably broken while I was being born."

"Oh," Eleni said, shocked such a thing could happen.

"But kind folks brought me all the way up to Tobermory so Dr. MacReady could care for me," Iona continued. "And after he did all that he could, he asked Miss Dundonald to take me in until I was stronger. And we grew to love one another, so I have never left Aros."

"You . . . are . . . her . . . baby," Eleni said, pronouncing each word carefully.

Iona beamed approval at Eleni's progress. "That's right. And now, you are my friend." Iona pointed from Eleni to herself and then put her hand over her heart.

"Friend," Eleni echoed, and then slowly, she understood what Iona was telling her. "Friend," she repeated, smiling. *"Ystävä."*

"'Oos-sta-vah,'" Iona repeated.

Eleni nodded. "And you are like *sisar* to me, little Iona," she whispered.

"'See-sar.' Why, it means 'sister,'" Iona said in English, looking startled for a moment. "Sister! Is that what you are calling me, Eleni?"

Eleni nodded, hoping—no, feeling certain—they were saying the same thing.

"Thank you, Eleni," Iona said, and she put her small white hand over her heart once more.

"Hello, girl," Col Hardie said to Eleni after church the next morning. He and his friends blocked the narrow walkway just outside the church door, but Col didn't seem to notice. Eleni's heart thumped in alarm, and she silently willed the other girls from Aros to draw near, because Miss Dundonald lingered in the small stone church. She was questioning the young, quaking minister about his sermon.

Eleni curtsied and looked down at her feet, pretending she could not understand him. "She's foreign. She doesn't know what it is you say, sir," Iona fibbed, her voice a mere peep. Behind her, Bethie, Moira, Pol, and Annie twittered like uneasy doves, but they stayed as close to Eleni and Iona as they dared.

"What's to understand?" one of Col's rough cronies said,

laughing. "Col fancies the foreign lass, and that's that. He can have what he wants on this island."

"Yes," another boy said. "His father doesn't care. He's busy with other things."

Col Hardie had stared hard at Eleni for weeks, people had noticed. Today, in church, he'd sat next to red-haired Angus Hume, who was a much nicer boy than Col ever was, Iona whispered to Eleni, even though Angus was a Sassenach. An Englishman. Angus's father had come to Mull a few years earlier to run the British Fisheries Society, the office of which was just opposite the pier.

But Col Hardie was the factor's son, and the factor—the absent laird's official agent—was a powerful man on the isle of Mull. Col seemed to have taken on some of his father's authority, now that most of the Macleans were scattered—in hiding since Culloden, some said—among the outer isles. Col was a wild young man, and his stride was long, and his laugh was confident and loud. He wore his black hair poofed up and twizzled forward into a glossy curl, and his skin was pink from his being out so much in the sun. His too-full cheeks were ruddy, and his too-full lips seemed always greedy for something good to eat or drink. As was his habit, Col wore his scarlet jacket with the brass buttons, though Miss Dundonald had once observed privately that it was not a proper garment for any lad to wear to church.

But where was Miss Dundonald now? Still busy grilling the minister, Eleni feared.

A few townspeople edged nervously past the silent group

of young people, because Col was known for his sharp tongue and quick temper. Two village girls eyed Col with admiration, though, and their mothers stared hard at Eleni, for say what folks might about the lad, he was a local force to be reckoned with. Any girl who married him would be well taken care of— for life. And their families would be, too.

Col frowned. "I think she knows what I'm saying," he announced loudly.

His rough friend laughed once more. "She's the bonniest lass on the island," he said, "and that's enough for our Col. He doesn't *need* her to talk."

"Better if she can't," a second loutish lad chimed in with a smirk.

*Sisu,* Eleni told herself, not looking up.

"Rest easy, Ewan. Easy, Douggie," Angus Hume said, blushing at his friends' crude words and bad manners.

"Why *should* we rest easy?" the second rough boy asked, blustering. "It's not as though these lasses are ladies, is it?"

"It's not as though they're *what*?" Miss Dundonald's voice boomed, ringing off the surrounding stones as she emerged from the church.

The young men—even Col Hardie—stepped back a pace or two. "Good day, Miss Dundonald," Col mumbled, for he had been bidden by his father always to show respect to the woman, Maclean that she was.

"Good day, Col Hardie. Now it's time for you lads to clear off and go home to your dinners," Miss Dundonald said, flapping her hands as if shooing away a few pesky chickens from her doorstep. "And stop pestering innocent, respectable, churchgoing girls, while you're about it."

"'Respectable girls,'" one of the louts mimicked under his breath as he turned away.

"Not for long," the other lout whispered—loud enough for everyone to hear. "Not if Col Hardie has anything to say about it!"

# Chapter Fifteen

## St. Agnes's Eve

"Here's the starch, miss," Pol said as she balanced the old chipped bowl on one hip while nudging open the door to the washhouse.

"Thank you," Eleni said, taking the bowl of thick, coarsely grated potato-and-water paste from her. She had been at Aros nearly six months now, and she was glad to have a job to do, as she was accustomed to working.

"Any sign yet of Ian Mackay?" Moira asked. The crotchety old fisherman was recovering from an injury to his foot, but he was fit enough—and thirsty enough for the Gull & Gherkin's spirits—to have agreed to work the laundry's new box mangle for the Aros girls on ironing day.

Pol paused on the doorstep and looked down the mist-hung path that led up from Tobermory Bay, it being a surprisingly soft January day on the isle of Mull. She squinted, then shook her head.

"He's late, but we'll be ready for him," Moira said firmly.

Eleni handed the bowl of potato starch to Iona, who was

standing at the ready at a long wooden table. Iona sniffed at the starch, and then smiled her approval of its freshness at a relieved Pol. She began sponging some of the starch onto the flat items they were ironing first that day, and then passed each one on to Bethie. The laundrymaid slipped these items neatly inside wide bedsheets that were folded small, in preparation for the mangle. Moira hummed under her breath as she used the long-handled charcoal ladle to stir the waiting coals.

The washhouse smelled of fresh sun-dried linen, grated raw potato, charcoal, smoke from the stove that warmed them and fueled and heated their irons, and of the sprigs of lavender Miss Dundonald tucked inside the finished sheets her laundry sent back into town. Eleni loved it when Miss Dundonald allowed her to help out on ironing day.

"I'm here," a man's self-important voice boomed out, and Ian Mackay hobbled into the cozy washroom, casting aside his jacket and rolling up his sleeves in preparation for the heavy work to come. Moira slid open the heels of two of the waiting irons, then ladled in the glowing coals she had prepared. Closing the irons, she lifted them gingerly by their hardwood handles and handed them over to Eleni, who began to iron.

Eleni's self-chosen specialty was the finishing work, a highly skilled task—much the same as she'd performed for Lady Sigrid, in Inkoo—that consumed most of her attention. But she had placed her tilt-topped ironing table so she could gaze out toward the harbor when the days were fine. As she worked, with Iona looking on in admiration, Eleni listened dreamily to Ian Mackay's complaints and muffled curses, to Moira's hum, and to Bethie murmur as she neatly folded the damp clothes. Eleni's thoughts floated somewhere above her, and her mind turned to Finland. To home.

But *was* Finland home, now? Perhaps only Matias would remember she had once lived in that fair country, Eleni thought sadly. And maybe even *he* had forgotten her, so much time had passed. Matias would be seventeen—to her fifteen—by now, Eleni reminded herself, and he was such a handsome lad, all the Helsinki girls had surely long ago taken notice of him. They would sway down the street in front of Matias on market day, or come into the shoemaker's shop on quickly invented errands, or cast sidelong glances in his direction before church on Sunday morning.

It made Eleni furious just thinking about it.

Or Matias might be fighting the Russians along the eastern border at this very moment, she thought suddenly, chilled. He might even be wounded!

"Careful," Iona warned, nodding toward the frill that Eleni was nearly scorching.

"Oh. *Kiitos*," Eleni said softly, but then she yawned, for she had not been sleeping well.

"Eleni, pay attention," Iona gently chided her. "There is still Mrs. Louden's sleeping gown for you to finish. And here's a hot egg iron for those flounces. I will tell you something wonderful, to keep you awake," she said suddenly. "Or else you will simply float away from us all."

"Something wonderful," Eleni said carefully. "Yes, please."

Iona leaned forward and lowered her voice. "Miss Dundonald is going to give us the dreaming eggs tomorrow night, for tomorrow is a special day," she said, and then she leaned back and smiled.

"Eggs?" Eleni asked, looking at the cooling egg iron in her hand.

"Not that kind of egg," Iona said, laughing. "I mean the kind we eat."

"Oh?" Eleni said, wondering what made this news so wonderful—although she liked eating eggs, and it was still a treat to have as many as she wanted for the first time in her life, courtesy of Aros's cheerful, obliging hens.

Iona frowned, trying to think where to begin. "See, Miss Dundonald has many old books in her library, right?" she asked, not waiting for an answer. "And she loves to read about the old time in Scotland, right? And one of the oldest stories is about St. Agnes's Eve, which is tomorrow night. January twentieth." Eleni nodded. "And if a maiden skips her supper and tea on St. Agnes's Eve," Iona continued earnestly, "and eats a dreaming egg, and then walks backwards to bed while reciting a special rhyme, she will dream of the man she is to marry."

Eleni sat back and stared at Iona, wondering if the little girl was teasing her. "Is this a pagan thing?" she finally asked, mostly because Iona seemed to be waiting for her to say something, anything.

"No," Iona said, shocked at the suggestion. "It's scholarly! Or a Catholic thing, I suppose. Only many of us haven't been Catholics around these parts for more than two hundred years, so I'm not sure we've got the spell completely right. It's an old custom, see."

Eleni frowned. "But—does Miss Dundonald want us to marry and leave Aros?"

The thought distressed her.

"Not at all," Iona assured her. "It's just that she is curious to see what will happen if we follow the instructions. Moira and Bethie and I tried it for the first time last year."

"And who will you marry?" Eleni asked, smiling.

Iona sighed. "Well, I dreamed about Duddy," she confessed reluctantly.

Eleni started to laugh. "You will marry a dog?" she asked. "Duddy is a very nice dog, Iona, but—"

"Maybe I said the rhyme wrong," Iona interrupted testily. "Or maybe I was just too young for the magic to work. But Moira dreamed about Ian Mackay," she reported, leaning forward as she whispered the news.

"She does not even like Ian Mackay," Eleni whispered back. "Why will she marry him? And Ian Mackay has a wife at home. What will the wife say about all this?"

"I suppose Moira's spell didn't work, either," Iona admitted, shaking her head in temporary defeat. "But Bethie dreamed about Willie the Post. And he's not married."

"Miss Dundonald does not like Willie the Post," Eleni said. "She says he tickles all the girls."

"Well, he's got to stop tickling them some day," Iona said, scowling.

Eleni thought about what Iona had told her. "How do we make these dreaming eggs?" she finally asked.

"Mrs. Lochiel and Pol will make them for us," Iona said. "They'll boil the eggs until they're hard, see—with two big fist-fuls of salt in the water so the eggshells come off nice. Then they'll take out the yolks and pack the eggs with salt. Then we girls will eat them tomorrow night, and we'll fall asleep and dream. But maybe you will dream about Col Hardie," Iona said, suddenly gloomy. "He followed us about in the village last week, you know."

"Oof," Eleni said, trying to ignore Iona's words about Col Hardie, for the young man scared her more than a little. "Hard egg and salt. I think I will dream that I marry a big glass of water."

"Eleni," Iona said, awed. "You made a joke—in Gaelic!"

Eleni shrugged modestly, but she was pink with pleasure, because she was proud of how far she'd come in learning two such difficult languages. "How do you say the rhyme?" she asked Iona, mostly to shift the little girl's attention away from herself.

"Oh, I've been studying it again—so I'd get it right this time," Iona told her. "Here it is in English, Eleni, so listen well.

*"Fair St. Agnes, play thy part,*
*And send to me my own sweetheart,*
*Not in his best or worst array,*
*But in the clothes he wears every day;*
*That tomorrow I may him ken,*
*From among all other men."*

"'I may him ken'?" Eleni asked, frowning with concentration.

"'*Ken*' means to know who he is," Iona said. "D'you think that you can learn the rhyme in time for tomorrow night, Eleni?"

"I will try," Eleni said, resuming her work. "Say the first lines for me one more time, please, Iona."

"*Fair St. Agnes, play thy part, and send to me my own sweet-heart,*" Iona recited.

*"My own sweetheart,"* Eleni echoed.

She already knew who she was going to think of when she said those words—and it wasn't Col Hardie.

St. Agnes's Eve was such a cold night that year that when Eleni finished cleaning her teeth with a fresh cherry-birch twig and looked out of her window before going to bed, the few lights visible around the curve of the bay in Tobermory looked like icy white smudges, rather than the glow from random candles or lanterns. The moon itself seemed to have been stretched out of shape by the cold, though there was no snow.

Able to stand the chill of her room no longer, Eleni wrapped a woolen shawl around herself, crept under her heavy covers, and tried to curl her stockinged feet around the stone bottle radiating heat at the foot of the narrow bed.

She would repeat the rhyme once more, slower this time, and without laughing, if possible, in case she had gotten some part of it wrong the first time she'd recited it. *"Fair St. Agnes, play thy part, and send to me my own sweetheart,"* she began, whispering the words. *"Not in his best or worst array, but in the clothes he wears every day; that tomorrow I may him ken, from among all other men."*

*Matias.*

What *were* the clothes that Matias had worn every day in Finland? Eleni closed her eyes and tried to remember. A thick linen shirt, and breeches, of course, and tall boots nearly as fine as those worn by any Swedish gentleman—for Matias's father had been a shoemaker, after all, before he was killed in that foolish, far-off war.

Oh, and Matias had worn his patchwork leather vest in all

seasons—under his long fur coat in winter, and sometimes over his bare brown chest in the summer.

Eleni tried to remember the vest's comforting, stirring smell. But she was hungry from skipping both supper and tea, and she was very thirsty from eating the salty dreaming egg, and it was difficult to concentrate.

*"Keh, keh,"* Eleni said softly, trying to unstick her tongue from her palate.

*"And what language is it you are speaking now, twilight child?"* an aggrieved voice asked.

Brounie! "Hello, sir," Eleni said, clutching the bedclothes around her shoulders as she strained to see him in the dark.

*"I've brought you some water,"* Brounie said, pushing an earthenware mug in front of him across the bedroom floor. *"Better drink it quick before it freezes. Never mind about me,"* he added under his breath.

Water! It sounded heavenly to Eleni, but she hesitated. After all, she thought, if she drank even a little of the water, just to be polite, she might have to make use of her chamberpot during the night. And it was far too cold a night for her to be getting out of bed and hoisting her nightclothes around her hips.

*"Lazy girl, drink,"* the brounie said, stomping his foot. *"I had to start worrying about lugging this mug all the way up the stairs the minute I saw you and the other girls eat those heathenish eggs in the kitchen, and I didn't go to all this trouble for nothing."*

Eleni hid her smile, but the thought of this stealthy little creature—a supernatural being himself, surely!—calling a blameless hard-boiled egg "heathenish" was difficult to fathom.

*"I know what you are thinking,"* Brounie said in a warning tone.

"I'm sorry," Eleni said, sitting up as best she could and reaching for the mug. The water in it was so cold that it seemed to burn as it went down her throat.

Brounie was letting her see him! A little, anyway.

*"Go ahead. Take a good look. Feast your eyes,"* he said, throwing his long arms into the air and posing in the moonlit room.

He *was* wee, Eleni saw, remembering what the brounie had told her about himself six months earlier, when she'd first arrived in Tobermory. The top of Brounie's surprisingly large head was just a bit taller than Eleni's bed. His body was stocky, though not fat, his short legs were bowed, his arms were sinewy and long, and his hands—though Eleni could see them only in silhouette, the room was so dim—looked big.

Most surprising of all, though, were the garments he wore: dainty embroidered house-slippers that looked as though they'd once belonged to a young Miss Dundonald, breeches made from the flower-sprigged curtain fabric used in her bedroom, suspenders fashioned from the same emerald green silken cord that tied back those very curtains, a shirt that looked to be made from the finest, thinnest, whitest linen Eleni had ever seen, and a squared-off pink satin cap.

The fanciest lace-trimmed undergarments in Miss Dundonald's clothes press—made to order during a long-ago trip to France with her mother, Eleni had heard—were fashioned from such pink satin. Eleni had seen those intimate garments while putting away Miss Dundonald's freshly laundered clothes.

*"Do not even phrase the question,"* the brounie said in his most quelling voice as he adjusted his satin cap. *"It is not as though*

*I am able to leave my chores undone and travel to the grandest tailor in Glasgow, is it? And Miss Dundonald will never give me new clothes to wear, because her books tell her I will leave Aros if she does. And am I one to let such costly stuff as I now wear be discarded simply because a certain person has grown larger around her middle?"*

"No, Brounie," Eleni said, biting her lips to hide her smile.

*"But my question is,"* the brounie said, as if Eleni had interrupted him midsentence, *"who are you going to dream about tonight? Pray, do not let it be me. Because I am destined to live alone, twilight child."* Brounie looked smug, not sad, when he said this.

"Then I will try not to dream of you," Eleni said meekly.

Brounie nodded sharply, and then settled on the floor, cross-legged, ignoring the cold—in spite of the fact that little puffs of steam accompanied his every word. *"It's a chancy custom, this dreaming of who you'll marry,"* he said casually, eyeing Eleni to see her reaction.

"Yes. And I do not even want to marry, for I do not ever want to leave this place, Brounie," Eleni said firmly. "It is now my home."

*"You will take your true home with you wherever you go,"* Brounie said. *"For your gifts are your home, now, twilight child. Not some dwelling place, however fine. And no one can take those gifts from you, once you accept what they are. As for the big lady wanting you to leave Aros, why, she does not,"* he added. *"But she can't resist trying out the old spell one more year. She's the curious sort, you see."*

"That is true," Eleni said, nodding.

*"And if there were young men at Aros,"* Brounie continued,

clearly trying to get around to saying something else, *"and if the custom were meant for them, then she'd be asking them to eat the salty eggs."* Eleni waited for him to say what was really on his mind. Brounie cleared his throat and adjusted his pink cap once more. *"And if this were a custom for young men,"* he said, *"I know of several in Tobermory who would try hard to dream of you tonight, Eleni Lavendyre. Or whatever your name is now."*

"Dream of me?" Eleni said, astonished. "But—but how do you know such a thing, when you never leave this house?"

*"Trust me, I have my sources,"* Brounie told her, proud. *"And as for me never leaving this house, why, even a shy creature of nervous disposition such as myself can lead a rich, full life."*

"Of course you can," Eleni was quick to agree. "And I'm certain that you do! But—what young man in Tobermory would wish to dream of me?"

*"Col Hardie, for one,"* Brounie stated flatly.

"No! Please, no, Brounie," Eleni said, almost begging as she spoke the words. "He would not dream of me. Why, look at me—with my hair so short, and this scar on my arm." She reached beneath her bedclothes and touched the length of it. It was nearly white now, and felt sunken and crumpled under her fingertips, though Dr. MacReady had done the best job possible mending her wound.

Brounie gave Eleni a rueful smile, for when she'd left for church that morning, the girl's chin-length hair gleamed white-gold beneath her lace-trimmed bonnet, and her cheeks glowed pink with health, and her waist nipped in so neat that it looked as if it might be the narrowest on the island. No wonder Col Hardie was after her! *"I was simply making an idle comment, twilight child,"* the brounie said, shrugging. He got stiffly to his feet. *"And now,"* he told Eleni, *"I must cease this chatter and get back to my domestic chores, which are many, and dull beyond belief."*

"We girls do try to leave things neat in the house," Eleni said meekly. "Surely there can't be *that* much work left to be done."

But Brounie shook his head sadly.

And then he was gone.

"Not Col Hardie, not Col Hardie," Eleni whispered just before falling asleep. "If I can't dream of Matias, then let me dream of—of red-haired Angus Hume, or that loathsome Ian Mackay, or even of Duddy. Though I wouldn't wish to steal him away from Iona," she added, smiling into her covers.

But it *was* Matias who walked into her restless dream that night, trailing the fresh air of a Finnish forest behind him.

In that dream, Eleni was almost too timid to look at Matias— her oldest friend—in his new guise as her future husband. But a sudden glimpse of the turn his brown, long-muscled forearm took sent a shiver up her spine that spread across the back of her head. And the plane of his cheek, and the straight line of his jaw made her turn away from him, shy.

For now Matias was a man.

# Chapter Sixteen

# A Last-Minute Guest

"At least that storm cleared," Iona said, gazing down at the bay. It was late March, and she and Eleni had paused, heading home from Upper Tobermory in the cart. They'd been delivering neat packets of laundry to those of Miss Dundonald's customers who lived on the hill behind the town's busy waterfront street.

"But it came up so fast, and with no warning," Eleni said, shivering, for the sudden storm—and the weird green sky that accompanied it—had reminded her of the storm eight months earlier that pounded the *Saari*'s deck in Tobermory Bay. "I hope no ships were lost during the night," she said, frowning.

"We would have heard," Iona said, patting her friend's hand in a motherly way. "Now let's go down the hill and have a wee look 'round in town before we have to get back to Aros. We're supposed to help prepare for Miss Dundonald's dinner party."

As the girls descended the hill, they looked down on a ribbon of low, steep-roofed buildings that seemed to unfurl around the busy bay. The town's buildings looked like a line of people standing arm-in-arm, Eleni sometimes thought. The curve of buildings was only one structure deep, and each house or business looked straight out at Tobermory Bay. There were no buildings at all on the bay side of the street, just a low whitewashed wall meant to keep people from tumbling off the road and onto the shingle on dark, rainy nights—or on boozy ones, Eleni supposed.

There was so much going on along the busy side of Tobermory's main street that Eleni and Iona never knew where to look first when going through the town. Nearly all of Tobermory's shops served more than one purpose, making them that much more interesting in the girls' eyes. For instance, the apothecary tended to Mull's poorer folk when they were ill, but he also sold everyone in town their restorative powders or potions, or rock candy, which had the benefit of being both a medicine and a sweet. And his wife trimmed hats.

The provisions shop was where an islander could buy such everyday items as sugar, tea, or coffee, or, splurging, purchase more exotic, imported things such as cinnamon, quinine, molasses, or ginger—but it was also the place a sailor could buy rope or tobacco, or even get his hair cut, if he'd been a long time at sea.

The butcher sold cured bacon and fresh meat, of course, but he also sold pickles and bait, and the cheese shop sold French corsets and finely embroidered handkerchiefs in addition to cheese. Tobermory's dress goods shop sold a dizzying variety of cloth—twenty-seven kinds, at last count, according to Moira and Bethie—but they also sold ribbons, costly looking glasses from London, and books, when they could get them.

And the shop served coffee and spice biscuits to the women who shopped there.

Tobermory was a much visited little town, due to its busy harbor, and so the Gull & Gherkin had rooms upstairs to let, as did the small inn, the saddlery shop, the county bank, the brewer's shop, and the baker's shop, too—which also roasted poor folks' meats and boiled their puddings. In fact, the only two establishments that didn't conduct additional business were the British Fisheries Society and the church.

Eleni and Iona both liked visiting the dress goods shop best, but Fancy was tired that afternoon, having plodded up and down Upper Tobermory's winding lanes. So when Iona tried to guide the pony to the side of the road in front of the dress goods shop, Fancy kept going as if no command had been given.

"Oh, let Fancy walk on, poor thing," Eleni said, feeling sorry for the shaggy animal. "We will stop here some other day, Iona."

"She can speak!" a triumphant voice cried out from the doorway of the British Fisheries Society. "I thought as much." It was Col Hardie, and he stepped into the road, grabbed hold of Fancy's bridle, and gave the girls a showy bow. Angus Hume was right behind him, looking as if he wanted to apologize to Eleni and Iona in advance for whatever might happen next.

"Good afternoon, sir," Eleni murmured, for it was no longer any use pretending she could not understand him.

Beside her, Iona scowled, and she tugged at Eleni's arm. "We must go," the little girl whispered. "*Walk on,* Fancy," she said, giving the reins a shake. But Fancy stood still, not knowing what to do. She shook her heavy head, then lowered it, waiting.

"Good afternoon, Eleni Lavendyre," Col said, mimicking her slight accent. "So you Aros girls would let a pony get the better of you," he said, laughing. "What's next? Taking orders from a kitten?"

Iona froze and then looked straight ahead as if nothing were wrong, but Eleni forced herself to meet Col Hardie's challenging gaze. "Please, sir, let our pony go," she said to him. "They wait for us at home."

"But you had time enough to stop before the pony told you no," Col argued, softening his voice as he tried to tease. "Step down and bide a wee, why don't you? Angus and I will buy you a treat. And the little lass, too. Why, I'll pay some lad to hold your pony's bridle, if you're afraid she'll trot back to Aros without you."

"We're not afraid of *anything*," Iona called out in a trembling voice. But still, she would not look at Col Hardie.

"Come on, Col," Angus muttered, blushing as he tugged at his friend's red jacket. "You're scaring them."

Col held his hands up in the air, as if to show Eleni and Iona he meant no harm. "I was only trying to help these lassies—and to buy them a treat. Was that so wrong?" he asked the small crowd that by now was watching his every move and hanging on each word. "Perhaps I should come a-calling at Aros, instead," he suggested loudly, looking straight into Eleni's green eyes.

A few folks murmured amongst themselves, hearing these words, for Col Hardie belonged to a rich and powerful family, and Eleni Lavendyre was just a girl who'd fallen off some foreign ship—a battered vessel much like the one pulling up to the pier just now, its ragged mainsail flapping in the stiff afternoon breeze. Men working on the pier scurried to secure the ship's lines, and one young sailor wearing a vest under his quilted linen jacket jumped onto the pier to help.

"Col Hardie has offered to call on the lass," people in the street opposite the pier whispered to one another. "Why would he do such a thing, him being who he is and all? And what will his father say?" "But just look at her," other folks argued. "So bonnie and fair."

"Please, sir, you must *not* come to Aros," Iona cried angrily, near tears. "Else our dog might bite you!" Eleni did not understand why Iona would say such a false thing about gentle Duddy, but she did not contradict the little girl.

For the first time, Col Hardie looked taken aback, and then he became angry, as some of the murmurs coming from the edge of the road turned to muffled laughter.

"Thank you for holding Fancy for us, sir," Eleni told Col, praying hard that her voice would not break. "It was a kindness. But we must go home now, or Miss Dundonald will worry." Col's expression softened, hearing Eleni's soothing and respectful words. He stepped away from the pony cart, shrugging to show how little any of this mattered to him. But Angus Hume shot Eleni a grateful smile.

"Walk on," Iona said again, shaking the reins again—and this time, Fancy obeyed.

"I think Col Hardie was only trying to be friendly, Iona—but he does not know how," Eleni whispered as the cart creaked and groaned along the bumpy road that wound its way toward Aros's lane.

"Don't you dare start to like him, Eleni," Iona told her

fiercely. "Much less feel sorry for him. Not after what he did to Duddy." Eleni's eyes opened wide. "That's right, to *Duddy*," Iona said. "You've seen the dog's scar, of course?" she asked, and Eleni nodded. She had. It ran the entire length of his belly, and it was a terrible thing. "Well," Iona said, "Col Hardie just as good as put that scar there himself, up on Sgurr Dearg."

Eleni looked confused. "Sgurr Dearg?"

"That red peak down near Duart Castle, where our Miss Dundonald was born," Iona explained. "It's where Col Hardie went to slay the last wild boar on the island."

"What's a wild boar?" Eleni asked as the cart joggled along.

"It's a great fearsome pig, Eleni—as big as a man, some-times, and with razor-sharp tusks that can grow this long," Iona said, dropping the reins for a moment to hold her hands much farther apart than her own narrow shoulders.

Eleni stared at Iona, hardly able to believe what she was hearing.

"Col Hardie heard the boar had been spotted," Iona said, "and he grabbed the Maclean's ghillie and the estate's best dog—Duddy, of course—and off he went. And Col was only fourteen at the time, but the ghillie didn't dare tell him no."

"But Duddy used to herd sheep, not hunt pigs," Eleni said, confused.

"He *did* herd sheep. And he was famous for it," Iona exclaimed. "Why, a shepherd never had to say a word of command, not when Duddy was on the job! He would nip and bark, and his energy never flagged. Duddy could give eye to the stupidest sheep and it would obey his every wish. He was the most valuable dog on the island, Eleni. Everyone said so! But Col thought the dog might distract the boar just long enough for him to kill it, and the ghillie would be his witness to this *brave deed*," she said, sneering. "Col Hardie wanted to be everybody's hero, that's what *he* wanted."

"But—what happened?" Eleni asked.

Iona shrugged to show her disgust. "Well, there *was* a wild boar up the mountain, it turns out, and Duddy went after it, probably thinking he was protecting Col and the ghillie from the ravening creature."

"Oh, no," Eleni said, almost breathing the words.

"Oh, yes," Iona said. "And while the boar was slashing Duddy's belly wide open from stem to stern, Col missed his aim. But the ghillie refused to leave the wounded dog behind, no matter how many threats Col made to him. So Col stormed off home alone," the little girl continued, "and the ghillie wrapped poor brave Duddy in his plaid, guts and all. He slung him over his back and carried him down the hill. And then he borrowed a shepherd's cart and drove it all the way from Craignure up to Tobermory so Dr. MacReady could stuff everything back inside Duddy and stitch him up. Why, it was a miracle Duddy lived! And the whole thing was Col Hardie's fault, and the ghillie made sure everyone knew it, and now you know the story as well. So you must not ever say you like Col." And Iona leaned back, satisfied to have told Duddy's tale.

Eleni could barely breathe, she was so angry.

"And Col even tried to get the ghillie thrashed for being disobedient to him," Iona added, her brown eyes flashing. "But *that* never happened. And Col found out soon enough how angry folks were with him—mostly for ruining a valuable dog, of course, for poor Duddy could never work again. And that's what people care about on Mull."

"But—but why is everyone so respectful of Col Hardie now, when they know this story?" Eleni asked, confused.

Iona shrugged once more. "That was four years ago, and even Miss Dundonald says you can't stay angry with someone for long. Not when you live on an island."

It must be a little like not fighting aboard ship, Eleni thought, remembering what happened between Pekka and Akseli, and where that had led.

The cart made its slow way up the path that led to Aros, and Eleni thought about Col Hardie and what he had done. All folks made mistakes, she told herself—*especially* when they were young. But people could change! Hadn't Col Hardie just attempted to show them a kindness, even if he had been clumsy about it?

He was like Pekka, perhaps—just awkward, and even a little bit shy.

Still, Eleni argued silently, to hurt a dog! And not just any dog, but Duddy. Maybe Col was more like Akseli than he was like Pekka. That was a frightening thing to think about. "Thank you for telling me, Iona," Eleni said as they neared the big house.

"Well, I thought it was a thing that you should know," Iona said, sounding a little prim. "And so now you do."

"We ate so many salted oysters when I was a girl that I thought I'd grow a shell," Moira said two hours later in Miss Dundonald's fragrant kitchen. She was stirring spirit-soaked raisins into the plum pudding batter as Pol held the bowl steady. Moira's frizzy hair quivered with her effort. "There were lots of 'em about, see, so they were cheap," she said.

"Ugh. Oysters," Bethie said, making a face. "We et mostly bread and onions, but at least those grew on God's good earth," she said, scooping up caper berries from a stone bottle with a long-handled spoon. "And we had cheese and bacon sometimes, too, so I guess we were luckier than you, Moira. What did you eat in Finland, Miss Eleni?"

"Yes—tell us what you used to eat, miss," Moira urged.

Eleni smiled. "Well, when I was small," she began, "my mother and father fed me fish that he caught in the sea, and bread, and good cheese. Clean Finnish food. And we gathered blueberries in the forest every summer," she added, wishing that she had a bowl of them to eat that very minute. "We dried them, and ate them all through the winter to help us stay healthy and strong."

"And what about when you were living with Lady Sigrid?" Iona asked, her legs dangling as she sat on the rush-bottomed stool watching the dinner party preparations, for Dr. MacReady—and a last-minute guest, he'd told Miss Dundonald by messenger—would be arriving in only three more hours. "What did you eat at the Lady Sigrid's house, Eleni?" The little girl loved hearing about the years Eleni had spent working for the Wallibjörns in Inkoo. After all, Eleni had been the same age when she started working there as Iona was now, and Eleni knew how to make even the dullest evening spent kneading Lady Sigrid's bumpy feet sound funny.

"With Lady Sigrid, I ate food almost as grand as the food we eat here at Aros," Eleni reported, checking the leg of mutton that was boiling on the stove. "But we ate *pulla* sometimes, too, and other sweet breads. It was very nice."

"I love sweets," Bethie said with a dreamy look on her face.

Moira laughed. "We all do, Bethie. But we'll never be spooning up Mrs. Lochiel's best stewed fruit or eating her plum pudding if we don't get busy."

"That's right," Mrs. Lochiel said, bustling into the kitchen with the platter of cold poached salmon she'd fetched from the north-facing larder. "Eleni, I need for you and Iona to get out from underfoot. Go and help Annie prepare the table, will ye? She gets all flusterpated when we have guests."

"That she does," Pol said eagerly. "Why, the last time Dr. MacReady came for afternoon coffee, Annie cut up the cake before she even handed it around. Like she was afeared the doctor would take too much, else, or maybe gobble the whole thing down! And Miss Dundonald was angry with Annie for the insult to her friend. Well," she added after thinking about it for a moment, "as angry as she gets, leastways."

When the village clock chimed eight, and the dining table was perfect, and dinner was cooked, and every candle and downstairs fire at Aros burned bright, Eleni, Iona, and Duddy joined Miss Dundonald in her pretty drawing room to await their guests. Mrs. Lochiel, Annie, Pol, Moira, and Bethie would be feasting in the kitchen, though all but Mrs. Lochiel were to take turns serving, they'd decided. Each girl wanted to get a glimpse of what was going on in the dining room—for Dr. MacReady was bringing a guest, and it was unusual for a stranger to be invited to Aros for dinner.

"Dr. MacReady says you'll be able to converse in Swedish with his friend," Miss Dundonald whispered to Eleni, squeezing her hand. "That will be nice for you, dearie."

Swedish! Eleni bit her lip and hoped she would be able to remember enough Swedish words to carry on a polite conversation, although only a year ago she'd spoken that language every day. But now, "A new day shows a new way," as Äiti had always so bravely said.

A full minute before even the sharpest human ear among them heard the crunch of carriage wheels upon gravel, Duddy cocked his head, listening. "They're almost here," Miss Dundonald said, smiling broadly.

And a moment later, there stood Dr. MacReady—with a handsome young man by his side.

"Here's that Miss Lavendyre I was telling you about, laddie," Eleni just barely heard Dr. MacReady say.

And then she crumpled onto the floor in a faint—right at Matias's feet.

# Chapter Seventeen

# The Little Lake
# of the Green-Clad Women

"**D**on't frighten our poor Eleni, or she might faint again," Iona called over her shoulder to Matias as she limped gamely along, her dark braids flapping as she led the way down a barely-there forest path. Matias looked as though he wanted to pick up the child and throw her over his shoulder so the three of them could move more quickly, but instead, he glanced back and flashed Eleni a teasing smile.

"That was more than four weeks ago, Iona," Eleni said, ignoring Matias as best she could. She didn't want to grumble, but really! What did Miss Dundonald and Dr. MacReady, or Matias, for that matter, *think* would happen, surprising her the way they had?

Although to be fair, Matias hadn't known she would be at Aros, having been told only that a "Miss Lavendyre" would probably enjoy chatting with someone in decent Swedish, for a change, and the food would be good.

And Miss Dundonald knew only that the young foreign sailor, Dr. MacReady's friend, was back in Tobermory unexpectedly due to the freakish storm of the night before.

"You fell like a rock," Iona said, parting the bushes to reveal the *lochan*.

The hidden lake sparkled bewitchingly in the thin April sunshine. It was called Lochan nam Ban Uaine, "The Little Lake of the Green-Clad Women."

"It's named for the fairies who live around here," Iona informed Eleni and Matias, pleased in advance, and she waited for their awed response.

"Fairies!" Matias exclaimed, laughing. "Eleni will feel right at home, then." He glanced at Eleni and grinned, looking much like the boy he used to be—though he had grown very tall and strong, and his face and arms were even browner than before, from his years at sea. But his gold-brown hair still curled against his neck, Eleni noticed shyly, and his blue eyes sparkled, and his broad, good-humored smile seemed to split his face in two when he was happy—which seemed to be most of the time, lately.

"*Shhh,*" Eleni said, glancing at her young friend, because she did not want Iona to be told any of the old stories about her.

But the little girl was staring at the pretty lake. "Look, Eleni," she whispered. Brilliant blue dragonflies skimmed low over the round *lochan*, dipping their bottoms into the water's edge. Rhododendrons crowded its banks, and waterlilies clustered on its surface—like enameled jewels, Eleni thought, unable now to look away. The sun slanted across the lake, the water's surface rippled from Duddy's eager explorations, and light turned its shallow parts transparent. The water was a beautiful amber-brown, like clear tea, Eleni marveled. A little lighter than Iona's sparkling eyes.

"Follow me, you two," Iona said, working her way through

the brush. "There's a perfect place to sit just over there. It's a fallen log covered with moss as thick as velvet," she said, relishing the luxurious, grown-up sound of the words.

"You've been here many times before?" Matias asked.

"Not *many* times," Iona admitted. "And not at all since Eleni came to Tobermory," she added over her shoulder as she hobbled along the barely visible path. "But Duddy and I love the *lochan*, and Moira and Bethie won't come anymore, so I decided we three should be the ones to visit it again."

"Why won't Moira and Bethie come here?" Eleni asked, although she knew that the laundrymaids preferred town to country, given a day off.

"They said they felt the *drawing*," Iona told her, only half scoffing. "Of the fairies," she explained, seeing their expressions. "They draw you to them, see, and the next thing you know, you're shut up in a cave for a hundred years or more."

Matias shot Eleni a secret look and waggled his fingertips as if casting a spell on her. *"I will take you under the earth,"* he whispered, clearly not intimidated by Scottish fairies, however irritable they might be.

"Stop that, Matias," Eleni whispered in Finnish. "Do not anger them—or hurt little Iona's feelings." But then she couldn't help but giggle, seeing Matias's expression.

"'Tisn't funny, Eleni," Iona scolded. "The fairies *will* take you, if you mock them."

"But why would they want to do that?" Eleni asked, looking around a little nervously, in spite of herself. For it seemed obvious, as Matias was implying, that if there really were Scottish fairies, they were not at all like Finland's *keijukainen*, the tiny, wish-granting forest sprite a much younger Eleni had once called "little bird."

"They'd do it just to cause mischief," Iona said softly. "Oh, here's the place I remembered," she said, gesturing toward a length of slowly rotting wood. "Sit," she told Eleni and Matias, and the three of them sat gingerly down. "And Duddy," Iona called out bossily, "don't stray too far."

"Don't they mind it when Duddy pounces all around?" Eleni asked softly, trying to keep an eye on the dog's black tail as he disappeared behind a bush.

"No. The fairies seem to like him," Iona said, shrugging away this little mystery. "And he likes them, too."

Matias stretched out his long, lean legs and crossed his ankles, obviously enjoying his day off. He *had* worked for a shoemaker in Helsinki after his father had been killed, he'd told Eleni weeks earlier, but only for a year. Then his mother died, and he'd decided he would be better off working aboard a ship than trying to become a shoemaker himself, and doing badly what his father had done so well.

Jobs aboard ships were plentiful in the busy Helsinki harbor, even for boys, and Matias was lucky enough to find himself working for a kind Swedish captain who treated him well. The crewmembers were from many different countries, and Matias had learned Gaelic and English. He learned even more when the captain put him ashore at Tobermory three years ago for a period of several months, when he, Matias, was afflicted with a fever and a rattling cough that would not go away. Dr. MacReady had taken care of him.

Finding Matias to be an intelligent, agreeable, and interesting companion, Dr. MacReady invited him to stay in his own spacious home until his ship returned to Tobermory. The doctor's excellent housekeeper nursed young Matias back to health with double-yolked eggs, endless bowls of beef tea, and plates of sugar-dusted shortbread.

Now, Matias had finished his five years' service aboard the Finnish vessel, although prior to the storm his ship was meant to end up in London, not Tobermory. But upon landing, he'd decided to take some weeks off, helping Dr. MacReady however he could while planning what next to do with his life. He wanted to return the good doctor's favor. Dr. MacReady was urging Matias to stay on with him indefinitely as his apprentice, and to learn to put his already strong healing instincts to good use on Mull, which needed another doctor.

Eleni desperately wanted Matias to make his permanent home in Tobermory, but she couldn't think of a way to tell him so without appearing too bold.

"Let's see what Mrs. Lochiel packed for us to eat," Iona said, unwrapping the large parcel of food the cook had sent off with them.

"I won't say no," Matias said, peering into the fabric-wrapped parcel.

"Matias has never missed a meal," Eleni teased, but it was her own stomach that gurgled shamingly as she saw the tall stack of cress-and-cheese-and-butter sandwiches, the crumbling scones, and the thick slabs of apricot cake arrayed before them.

"We'll leave a wee bit here for you-know-who," Iona said matter-of-factly, sprinkling generous pieces of her scone behind the log.

Eleni added part of her sandwich to the fairy offering, and a broadly smiling Matias contributed an almost invisible pinch of his apricot cake. "That should fill the little terrors' bitty stomachs up," he whispered to Eleni in Finnish. "If such creatures even *have* stomachs, that is. I'll need to ask Dr. MacReady about that, for he's a man of science, and he would know such a thing."

"*Shhh,*" Eleni whispered again, nudging him, and feeling a little cross. For what would Matias say, she wondered, if she told him she had been able actually to speak with Tonttu, back in Inkoo, and with the blue men of the Minch, and with Brounie—and they with her, as well? She dared not tell him! But these generous beings, her honorary kinfolk, had helped her to survive thus far, Eleni knew.

The three young people became drowsy after finishing their meal, and Eleni felt her eyelids begin to close. She wanted badly to lean against Matias's once-familiar shoulder, to nestle her head against his leather vest, and then to rest as she would have done when they were children back in Finland. But only because this would be a comfortable place to take her ease, and for no other reason, Eleni told herself sternly. For this new Matias was almost a stranger to her, and she felt shy. He had been on his own for years, after all, and he'd sailed to lands she had never heard of, and he had probably met girls—or even women!—in those lands who were so beautiful he could never forget them. Perhaps Matias longed only for the day he could return to those women once more. Eleni sighed.

"What is wrong, Eleni?" Matias asked, keeping his voice low so as not to disturb Iona, who was slumped against his chest like a baby. She was fast asleep, although not a single hair on her sleek dark head was mussed.

"Why, nothing at all," Eleni said in Finnish, sitting up as straight as she could. "I was just trying to stay awake. Perhaps this place *is* enchanted, I feel so sleepy."

"Well, if you don't know if the lake is infested with fairies or not, then no one does," Matias said, laughing softly. "But if you were to ask me, with the vast medical knowledge I almost have, I'd say that what you are feeling now is the mystical enchantment of a long walk, a full stomach, and a warm day. Come lean against me, *tyttö*, like you used to do back home," he added, holding out his arm invitingly.

*Tyttö*. Girl! That was all she was to him, just another bossy little girl like Iona. "No, thank you, Matias," Eleni said stiffly. "I—"

"Duddy," Iona squawked, waking up suddenly and spotting the dog a third of the way around the lake. "Come back here at once, or the fairies will coax you away to their horrible cave!"

The dog ignored her, of course, as he was sniffing at the water's edge, and so Iona hobbled after him, obviously intending to drag him back to the mossy log by the scruff of his neck. And Eleni and Matias watched her go. Matias lowered the arm that had almost gone around Eleni's shoulder. He sighed, too, and frowned a little.

"Is it—is it very dull for you here in Tobermory, Matias, after having been at sea?" Eleni asked, feeling suddenly even more awkward around him than she had before.

Matias smiled once more, then shrugged. "It is a little dull *right now*," he said, giving Eleni a teasing look. "But most days the doctor keeps me busy, which I like. And some dullness in this life can be a good thing, as you yourself must know by now, little Eleni."

"I am not *so* little," Eleni said, sitting up straight once more. "I will be sixteen years old come *Juhannus,* and—"

"But they will not celebrate *Juhannus* here in Scotland," Matias interrupted, reminding her. "Not in the same manner as the Finns and Swedes did in Inkoo, anyway. I will help you make the day of your birth memorable, though, do not fear. Perhaps I will drop a spider in your hair to celebrate—or even a whole handful of them!"

Eleni turned to glare at him. "I am no longer a child, Matias," she told him.

"Or maybe I'll rig a bucket of water to fall on you when you open the door," Matias continued, ignoring her protests. "And then you can jump on my back once more and tell me you hate me to pieces."

"I never said that," Eleni objected, blushing.

"You did, you know," Matias said, nodding his head.

"But—does this mean you will still be living in Tobermory come summer?" Eleni asked, acting as if this were the most casual of questions. "Or do you miss the sea too much to stay here with such dull folk as we, here on the island?"

"Miss the sea?" Matias said, laughing. "It is a most tedious life, Eleni—except when you are *fighting* for your life. No, I do not miss the sea at all."

Eleni looked into his eyes and tilted her head. "And yet you do not know if you will remain on Mull," she stated, feeling suddenly certain she was right.

Matias sighed once more. "Try hiding anything from you, twilight child," he said with a rueful smile.

Eleni matched his smile. "I am sorry to disappoint you, dear Matias, but I do not mind being called by that name anymore," she said, lifting her chin proudly. "At least, not by you—and perhaps one or two others. But can you tell me why you might leave?" she asked, challenging him.

Matias shrugged again, but helplessly, as if not sure how best to explain his feelings. "Do you remember how angry I used to be with the Swedes, Eleni?" he finally asked. "For always telling us Finns what to do, and when to do it?"

Eleni nodded.

"Well," Matias said slowly, "I can't see that it's much different with the English and the Scots. Finland is not now a good place for the Finns, and this might be true of Scotland for the Scots as well, thanks to their new masters since Culloden, the money-minded English. Perhaps it is a good time for people to be leaving Tobermory. To be leaving this island."

"To be *leaving*? But—but Mull is my new home, Matias," Eleni said, her heart pounding. "So many bad things could have happened to either one of us along the way, but they didn't," she added, desperate for him to listen, to understand. "We were *spared*, Matias! And now we both have fine homes here in Tobermory, if we want them, and decent work to do, and—"

"Eleni! Matias!" Iona said, running back to the moss-covered log where they were sitting, with Duddy close behind her. "Someone is watching us."

"Is it the green-clad fairies?" Matias asked, smiling so that only Eleni could see.

Leaves rustled suddenly at the far edge of the lake, and three small, twittering birds took off across the still water. Duddy paused, turned his head, and growled.

"*Is* it the fairies, do you think?" Eleni asked Iona, thinking that perhaps she had been too distracted by Matias to sense their presence. For they must surely know she was here!

"No," Iona whispered, shaking her head. "Duddy would never growl at *them*. It's a mortal who's been spying on us, and he's been here the whole time, across the lake. I saw a flash of scarlet just now, between the trees. And that means it's Col Hardie, Eleni," the little girl added in a frightened whisper.

"Col Hardie?" Matias asked.

"I don't see anyone," Eleni said, her heart pounding.

"*I* did, though," Iona said, "and Duddy did, too. Let's go home," she said loudly, gathering up their things. "Miss Dundonald will be waiting for us, and we mustn't keep her."

"But—I love it here," Eleni said, murmuring her objection so softly that no one—*almost* no one—could hear.

"Perhaps I love it here, too," Matias said, and he looked at Eleni with eyes that were as bright as the enchanted lake itself.

# Chapter Eighteen

# Sisters

And suddenly, Col Hardie was everywhere. He strutted down Tobermory's main street just as Eleni and Iona finished making their deliveries. He laughed and boasted with friends outside the Gull & Gherkin's red door when the girls from Aros took their exercise after dinner on mild evenings. He galloped his spirited horse past poor plodding Fancy when Eleni and Iona were exploring the glens near Tobermory on free Saturday or Sunday afternoons. He was around every corner.

Soon, everyone on the island of Mull—including Matias— knew Eleni Lavendyre was the girl Col Hardie was interested in.

That foreign lass was leading Col Hardie on, some folks said—usually the people with daughters both ready and eager to marry a young man such as he, from such a prosperous family. Others whispered that Miss Dundonald's latest ward would end up in a bad way, parading her fair-haired beauty throughout town the way she did. The local lads couldn't be blamed if they followed her around. Bees sought out flowers, did they not? And perhaps the girl wasn't quite the same as other mortals, other people murmured. She spoke the Gaelic so strange, after all, and hadn't she been seen scattering food for the fairies near the little *lochan*?

Could young Col be blamed for being enchanted with her?

"He's going to ruin everything for us," Iona said one night while Eleni was combing the girl's gleaming dark hair, which was wavy from having been in braids all day.

"Who, Col Hardie?" Eleni asked, counting the strokes. "But *how* will he ruin things? Sorry," she murmured gently, as Iona winced. "I'm trying not to pull."

Iona's brown eyes flashed. "Well, first," she said, "he's spoiling our outings. You never know where he'll pop up next."

"From this day on, we will pretend we don't see him," Eleni said, liking the idea. Finished with her combing, she arranged Iona's pretty hair across her narrow shoulders like a fan.

"How do I look?" Iona asked shyly.

"You look like a very small princess," Eleni told her, beaming. And it was true, for the little girl's solemn visage and lace-trimmed sleeping gown did indeed make her look quite regal.

Iona sighed. "Perhaps," she said. "Until I stand up and begin to walk, that is. And then I look like the buffoon at the village fair." Her little mouth turned down in a frown.

Eleni felt ill, hearing these words. "Iona," she said, shocked. "Please do not say such bad things when it is a miracle you live at all."

"But it's true, about the way I walk," Iona said, her straight brows lowering and her face clouding—for, as Eleni had learned, the little girl's mood could change like the tide. "That's why no boy will ever love me," she added, sounding sad. "And that's why Col Hardie will ruin everything, because he's going to take you away, and then we won't have each other anymore. I'll be left all alone."

"I will never marry Col Hardie. And you will always have me, Iona," Eleni said quietly.

"How? If you're living in someone else's house?" Iona asked bitterly.

"You will come visit me often, and stay for months—no matter where I live," Eleni said, knowing somehow that she spoke the truth. "Or I will learn how to write better just so I can send you letters. And Willie the Post will carry them. He'll tell everyone in town I've written to you. And probably what I wrote, as well!"

Iona considered what Eleni had said. "It won't be the same," she finally mumbled. But at least she wasn't scowling anymore.

Eleni sighed. "My own life has shown me that nothing ever stays the same, *sisar*," she said, tying Iona's sleeping cap firmly under her chin.

"We're sisters," Iona remembered sleepily, looking pleased.

"Sisters," Eleni echoed. "For always, little Iona. I promise you."

"I wouldn't fret about Col Hardie too much, Meg," Dr. MacReady told Miss Dundonald one early June evening as they took their refreshment on the lawn that sloped down from Aros toward Tobermory Bay. "Matias tells me Eleni doesn't even like him."

"Well, I *do* fret, Jamie," Miss Dundonald said, sounding a

bit peevish. "Nothing good will come from his infatuation, you know."

"Eleni might do worse than to marry Col, despite what Matias says," Dr. MacReady said, keeping his voice mild. "Although I must say, Matias is not at all pleased by the attention Eleni is getting. But I suppose it's natural for him to feel protective toward her. They're like brother and sister, after all."

"But—Eleni marry Col?" Miss Dundonald exclaimed. "She is not quite sixteen, from what she tells me. And he's a wild one, Col Hardie. Besides," she added, sounding bitter, "I don't think marriage is what Col has in mind for our Eleni Lavendyre."

"That could be true," Dr. MacReady admitted reluctantly.

"I'm not allowing Eleni to be plucked off the vine by the first scoundrel who happens to take a fancy to her," Miss Dundonald said with an indignant snort.

"Of course you're not," Dr. MacReady agreed hastily.

"But what should I do?" Miss Dundonald asked. "Should I talk to her about—about *life*?"

Dr. MacReady nodded, but then he paused. He obviously had something to say, but he was finding it difficult.

"Go ahead, Jamie," Miss Dundonald told him softly.

"It's just that it's very likely that one of the girls at Aros is going to *want* to marry someday," Dr. MacReady said. "To have her own family, you know."

"I know," Miss Dundonald said. "But until that day comes, I'll try to make a peaceful life for each of them at Aros. It's bound to be a more comfortable life here than they'd find elsewhere, even if they did marry—for times are only going to get harder here in Scotland, Jamie, now that England is showing her greedy hand. Why, with the Clearances, English lords are chasing crofters off the farms they've worked for hundreds of years. And for what? So's they can raise a profitable mess of pie-faced sheep or gallop around, hunting deer to their heart's content."

"Well, *I* know the girls are probably better off here with you, and *you* know that," Dr. MacReady said, sighing. "But still, the day might come."

"Aye," Miss Dundonald murmured, brave. "And when it does, I'll help each one of them all I can. The sorry thing," she added, "is that I think it will be Iona who yearns most for her own family. And she could manage it, Jamie—but she'll be the least likely ever to get an offer of marriage, islanders being as backwards as they are about limps, and babes being abandoned on holy islands, and such-like."

"Iona could manage the British Fisheries Society with one hand behind her back," Dr. MacReady said, laughing. "Say," he added, his eyes shining. "Perhaps Angus Hume will cast his eye her way one day! Now, he's a nice lad, for a Sassenach."

"And I'd give Iona a fine dowry, if she truly fell in love with such a one," Miss Dundonald said. "But I'm not going to pay some lout to marry Iona if there's no love there."

"No one's even suggesting such a thing, Meggie," Dr. MacReady murmured. "But as for Eleni Lavendyre, you must give her whatever chance she wishes to take."

"I will, Jamie," Miss Dundonald said. "I promise."

# Chapter Nineteen

# The Dundonald Tartan

Helping to clean the plaids was one of Eleni's favorite laundry jobs, although it was a strenuous one. Each plaid belonging to a grown man was so big it took both laundrymaids and a couple of helpers to handle it. But it was a beautiful day in mid-June, so all the girls at Aros—and a few helpers from town, as well—were hard at work.

A Scottish man of the islands fashioned most of his plaid into enough pleats to form a kilt, Eleni had learned, which he then wore belted around his waist, and he pinned the two loose ends together at his left shoulder. "But what does the man wear *under* the kilt?" Eleni had asked Moira and Bethie once, blushing a little.

"Oh, Miss Eleni," Bethie said, clasping her face and erupting into fits of giggles.

"Stop being so silly, Bethie," Moira said, sounding stern. "A man simply wears his longest shirt, Eleni, and then he pins its tails between his legs. But here's a bawdy English joke for you," she added, grinning naughtily as she switched languages.

"'Pray tell,' the Scottish lady asks, 'is anything *worn* under your kilt?' 'No, lady, do not worry,' the Scotsman replies. 'Everything under my kilt is in excellent condition!' Excellent condition, Miss Eleni! Nothing was *worn out*."

Eleni looked confused, not understanding English too well at the time. "But—I do not know what you are saying," she finally told Moira, who was gasping with laughter, overcome by her own wit.

"Oh, Moira," Bethie had said, wiping away tears of laughter. "You are *bad*!"

It was a busy morning in town, Eleni saw, smiling now as she remembered the old joke. She looked down on Tobermory from Aros's bluff. The proprietor of the Gull & Gherkin was sweeping his step, bonneted women hurried among the little town's busy shops, and fishermen's wives sat gossiping on the shingle while they mended torn nets, their husbands having long since headed out to sea for the day. A recent arrival to the pier, a passenger ship named *The Rambler of Leith*, was being readied for repairs.

Eleni turned back to her work, brushing hard at the mud Dr. MacReady had splashed onto his hunting plaid.

"Look at this fine sight," Miss Dundonald said some hours later, gliding up behind Eleni. "It does my heart good to see Aros wearing so many brave colors on her lawns and hedges once more. Right, Duddy?"

Beside her, Duddy wagged his tail.

Moira and Bethie had finished brushing the last plaid, and now four of the colorful woven lengths were stretched on the sweet-smelling lawn and over the stout hedges like oversized banners fallen from the sky. "Bring your brushes and buckets inside, everyone," Iona called out, beckoning them into the washhouse.

"Bide with me, Eleni Lavendyre," Miss Dundonald told Eleni. "I wish to speak to you." Shadows had begun to blur the edges of the lawn, but Miss Dundonald and Eleni were warm in the sunshine that remained. "It's a funny thing about clans, and family names," Miss Dundonald said after a few silent, brooding moments. "We're each given our father's surname, aren't we? Though we might never know him. Birth can be a mere accident, or so it seems. Why, look at Iona."

Eleni thought about the little girl.

"I will tell you something of my own past, if you'd care to hear it," Miss Dundonald said suddenly. "But only because there's a reason to tell you, mind. Once upon a time," she began, "there was a wee lass named Flora Maclean, who one day became my mother. She was orphaned when she was only eight years old, Eleni. Orphaned, like Iona—and like *you*. And Flora's uncle, 'the Maclean,' said she must come and live with his family at Duart Castle, right here on the isle of Mull. Down by Craignure, where the new road leads."

"I have heard of that place," Eleni said, thinking of the story Iona had told her about Col Hardie and the wild boar.

"And so Flora obeyed the laird and moved into the castle," Miss Dundonald continued. "But Flora grew up a little bit wild, though I hate to say it. She would roam the forests and hills as far as her long legs could carry her. And there was no one who could tell her what to do, she was such a headstrong lass. Not even the Maclean was her master," she said proudly, referring to the head of the clan.

Eleni liked Flora Maclean already.

"And then one day," Miss Dundonald said, leaning forward once more, "when Flora was about your age, just barely a woman, she met a handsome young man when she was out a-walking. And it was Fitzhugh Dundonald, a friend to the family and a tutor to young Lachlan Maclean, Flora's wee cousin."

"Mmm," Eleni murmured, imagining the scene.

"And so they stayed awhile in the woods," Miss Dundonald continued with some delicacy, "and they promised each other they would wed. They were thinking about how best to ask the laird when Fitzhugh was called home by his family—because of the 'forty-five."

That would be the 1745 Rising that led to the battlefield slaughter at Culloden early the next year, Eleni reminded herself hastily.

"And so Fitzhugh Dundonald left Duart in a great big hurry, and all too soon, poor Flora discovered she was going to have a wee baby," Miss Dundonald continued, pointing modestly to herself. "And Flora was an unmarried lass," she added, in case Eleni had forgotten that part of the story. Which she had not.

"And when the laird found out," Miss Dundonald continued, "why, he sent his men off to find Fitzhugh, and drag him back to do right by Flora and the Macleans, so the family would not be dishonored. But my father was dead, Eleni—killed at Culloden by the brutal English. And so the Maclean's men went to talk to the Dundonald people," she said, "and they told them what had happened. The Dundonalds settled some money on my mother, of course, which is how Flora Maclean came to buy the house at Aros for herself and for me, her wee baby daughter. But the family said I could be given the Dundonalds' name and claim their tartan."

"Oh," Eleni said with a sigh, much impressed by this romantic tale.

Miss Dundonald looked at her sharply. "Sad things happen every day to girls the wide world over, Eleni, and all for the love of a boy," she said. "It broke my poor mother's heart, though, that it did."

"But—why did Flora build a washhouse at Aros, if she was from two such grand families?" Eleni asked, for she'd long been wondering about this.

"Well, women have been washing clothes at the stream since God was a boy," Miss Dundonald explained. "But Mother decided she'd create something both useful and pretty here— because she was used to having things look spruce, I suppose. And she decided really to make a go of the place, just to spite the proud Macleans, I think. She told me once that *someone* in the family might as well do a useful job of work."

Eleni smiled at this, seeing where her own Miss Dundonald had gotten her spirit.

"And so Mother and I called Aros our home," Miss Dundonald continued, "and we made a garden, and we traveled whenever we could, and we had a very good life together. And when Mother died she left me Aros, of course, and I have continued to run the laundry. For that, and helping you girls, is *my* useful purpose in this life. But now there is another young girl on Mull who is facing trouble similar to my mother's."

"Who?" Eleni asked.

"You."

Eleni gasped. "Oh, no, Miss Dundonald. I would never shame you! I will stay here forever with you and Iona, and study hard, and help in the laundry, and—"

"No girl *means* to get herself in trouble," Miss Dundonald interrupted, shaking her head. "But fate—and a girl's own silliness—sometimes intervenes, Eleni. And I think Col Hardie believes he is to be your fate. He recently asked if he may come calling on you, my dear. It's an honor, folks say," she added, an unreadable expression on her face.

"But—but we *hate* Col Hardie," Eleni said, shocked at Miss Dundonald's suggestion. "He almost killed Duddy!"

"That was when Col was just a lad, Eleni," Miss Dundonald said, sighing. "As I hope my story taught you, we should not judge people only by the mistakes they make when they are young. I'm certain Col Hardie has learned a great deal since that sad day on Sgurr Dearg. His father is a decent man, after all, and Col might one day make you a very good husband." Miss Dundonald was trying hard to be fair.

"But I do not love him, Miss Dundonald!" Eleni exclaimed. "And Brounie said—" She bit off the rest of her sentence, but it was too late.

"Brounie?" Miss Dundonald whispered. "You have spoken to him, my dear?"

Eleni nodded, miserable. "Yes. Brounie is my friend, Miss Dundonald. Like Iona, and Matias, and like you."

"Thank you for that," Miss Dundonald said, though she still looked a bit stunned.

"And I should not speak of Brounie aloud," Eleni continued, "but he told me you do not want me to leave this place."

"Well, that is certainly true," Miss Dundonald admitted.
"But I have been told that you probably will, Eleni. Is it Matias
whom you fancy?" she asked after a moment. "I knew he was a
childhood friend, but I thought he was more a brother to you
than a sweetheart."

"I don't know yet who I *fancy*," Eleni said, pronouncing the
new word carefully.

Miss Dundonald smiled. "Well, 'I don't know' is a decision,
too, don't forget," she said, reaching over to pat Eleni's head.
"And you are wise to wait. My mother always told me the
French had it right with their old saying, 'There is no flirtation
in the bedroom.' And some women would say flirtation is the
most thrilling part of love! Why, just look at Dr. MacReady and
me. Though he *has* asked me to marry him in the past," she
added, looking proud and sad at the same time. "And more
than once."

"But you said no?" Eleni asked shyly.

Miss Dundonald lifted her chin proudly. "I thought perhaps
he was feeling sorry for me, when he asked. Because of my
mother and all," she explained. "But as for you, Eleni, you will
have a home with me here for as long as you want. Forever, if it
suits you. And I will tell Col Hardie not to come a-courting."

"Thank you, Miss Dundonald," Eleni told the woman.
"*Kiitos.*"

"So. You've spoken with the brounie!" Miss Dundonald
marveled, changing the subject as she looked at Eleni with
some curiosity. "Just imagine that. And have you seen him,

too, Eleni?" Eleni nodded. "What does he look like, dearie?" Miss Dundonald asked. "Tell me, do, for I've never seen him up close."

Eleni thought for a moment. "Well, he has a big head, and— he is a fine wee creature," she said, stumbling a little as she tried to describe her shy little friend. "But he dresses in clothes that are much too pretty," she added suddenly, glad Brounie could not hear the words she spoke. "It would be a good thing if you left some small man things around for him to wear, Miss Dundonald."

"Small man things?" Miss Dundonald repeated, her eyes sparkling.

"Yes," Eleni told her, nodding. "Like good linen for a new shirt, a *long* one, and soft leather for his house slippers, and— and maybe a plaid? The Dundonald tartan, he would like," she added, picturing Brounie dressed in such becoming attire.

"I cannot do that," Miss Dundonald said sadly. "Or the brounie will leave Aros forever."

"But that's not true," Eleni said. "Not for this brounie, anyway. He never wants to leave this place. I think the outside world makes him anxious."

"D'you think he would really wear new garments, if I set them out?" Miss Dundonald asked, blushing.

"Every day. He will love them!"

"Then consider it done," Miss Dundonald said, looking happier than she had in some time.

# Chapter Twenty

## Another Good-bye

"In what way would you like to celebrate your sixteenth birthday, Eleni?" Miss Dundonald asked as she, Eleni, and Iona sat on Aros's lawn just after evening tea.

And suddenly, Eleni knew. "I want to see Rubha nan Gall," she said softly. "You know, where my father's ship went down."

Miss Dundonald blinked her surprise at this somewhat morbid request, but she didn't object. Instead, she nodded her reluctant assent.

Iona frowned, however. "There's nothing left of the ship, Eleni," she said, fiddling with one of her long braids. "And its sailors are long since buried in the churchyard. There won't be anything to see."

"Oh, that's never true on the island," Miss Dundonald exclaimed. "Why, there will be birds galore out on the point. You might even spot some puffins! They haven't yet left for deep ocean, I hear."

Puffins—the very birds that the blue men of the Minch had told her to be kind to, Eleni thought, remembering the strange, feverish conversation that had surpassed the boundaries of language.

"Such colorful creatures, puffins are," Miss Dundonald said, shaking her head fondly, which set her heavy chins a-jiggling. "And good parents to their babies, too." She sighed, temporarily overcome by sentiment.

"What do puffins look like, Miss Dundonald?" Eleni asked. "How will I know them from all other birds?"

Miss Dundonald and Iona looked at each other and laughed. "You can't mistake a puffin for *any* other bird, dearie," Miss Dundonald finally explained. "You'll see."

*"It is your sixteenth birthday tomorrow, twilight child,"* Brounie said, bustling into Eleni's small bedroom some nights later, an hour after the household had retired.

Eleni opened her eyes, yawned, then sat up in the June half-light. "Yes, I know," she said, stretching. "Tomorrow is Friday, and it's *Juhannus*, and—why Brounie, what are you wearing?" she asked, peering at the small creature, who seemed extra shy tonight, and was obviously trying to act as though nothing about his appearance had changed the least bit.

But it had. Instead of silk-embroidered house slippers, Brounie wore black kidskin shoes laced up snug over his new white stockings. His collarless linen shirt looked both manly and made to order, it fitted him so well, and instead of his flowery breeches, Brounie wore a wee kilt fashioned from the gray, black, and white Dundonald plaid—probably cut down from an old shoulder sash that Miss Dundonald had worn on dress occasions, Eleni guessed. A gleaming leather belt cinched the kilt neatly around his stomach, which he seemed to be trying to hold in, and a new, squared-off cap fashioned from the same fine leather perched jauntily atop his blushing head.

*"I'm wearing the exact clothes I always wear,"* Brounie mumbled. *"And I thank you for them, child,"* he added in a barely audible aside.

It was all Eleni could do not to laugh out loud in delight. "Well, you look very bonnie, as you Scots say," she told him. "And I thank you for your early birthday greetings, sir."

*"You have been given a little holiday tomorrow, have you not?"* the brounie asked, settling himself cross-legged upon the floor in his usual fashion.

"I have," Eleni said, smiling in the gloom. "Iona and Matias and I have leave of our various studies and chores, and we're going to take the cart up to the bluff overlooking Rubha nan Gall. We three will have a picnic up there," she continued, excited. "Moira and Bethie were invited, too, but they said they prefer to help Mrs. Lochiel prepare a special dinner for tomorrow night."

*"To honor you,"* Brounie said, stating the obvious.

Now Eleni was the one to blush. "Yes," she admitted.

The brounie laughed. *"And think of your birthday last year, twilight child! You were on your father's ship somewhere in the Baltic, waiting for the wind to start blowing again and gazing up at the cloudless sky as if it might be able to tell you what would happen next in your life."*

"Was that where I spent my last birthday?" Eleni asked, surprised Brounie had knowledge of such a thing. "I couldn't tell one day from the other during that time. And I could never have *guessed* what would happen next in my life."

"*Any more than you can guess now,*" Brounie pointed out. "*Even though you are a twilight child,*" he added, examining one of his new shoes. He licked his thumb and wiped away a speck of dust.

"Oh," Eleni said, frightened for a moment as she thought of her future. "And—and have you come to give me a warning about what is to come, Brounie?"

The brounie shook his large head slowly, so as not to disturb his new leather cap. "*No. I canna do that, child. But I can give you this, both to help you remember your past and to celebrate your birth,*" he said, reaching under the folded-down top of one of his heavy stockings.

*It will be a dirk,* Eleni thought, for Miss Dundonald had told her that this small ceremonial knife was what Scottish men kept hidden and at the ready in their stockings.

"*It's not a knife, lassie,*" the brounie said, laughing as he scrambled to his feet. "*We can do better than that for your special day, I hope.*" And he handed Eleni a small wrapped packet that fit perfectly in the palm of her hand.

"Thank you, sir," Eleni said, bowing slightly in bed as she accepted the gift. Her fair hair tickled her shoulders as she inclined her head.

"*It's from the lot of us, and you may open it now,*" Brounie told her. He stood at ease next to her bed then, looking a little military, with his large hands clasped behind his back.

"From the lot of you?" Eleni echoed, unfolding the square of emerald green silk. "Oh," she exclaimed, staring at her birthday gift. A shining circle of intricately woven metals—bronze, silver, and gold—lay gleaming in her hand. An undulating wave made up of two thin strands of gold separated the maze-like bands that encircled a beautiful blue stone the exact color of Matias's eyes. The light from the stone seemed to jump like tiny *kokko* sparks around the darkened room.

"*Oh,*" Eleni said again.

"*Here's fine bronze sent from your prim sauna friend in Finland, see,*" Brounie told her, leaning over the brooch and pointing out a richly colored thread of metal. "*And here's gold that your brawny blue guardians gathered from the bottom of the Minch, and here's some of Scotland's finest silver, too,*" he added modestly, pointing out his own contribution. "*And the wee cunning clasp is from Duddy and the fairies at the little lake, though the fairies grumbled at the cost, of course, being a bit mean. And your mother and father searched forever to find this rare blue stone, though Pekka was the one who discovered it. And the strands of gold that make up the encircling wave are to symbolize your two sea voyages, and—*"

"My mother and father looked for this stone? And Pekka? And my *two* sea voyages?" Eleni asked, stunned by the brounie's confusing tumble of words. "But Äiti and Isä and Pekka are dead, Brounie," she said, her heart pounding. "And I have made only one sea voyage in my life. That was quite enough."

The small creature bit his lips together as if determined to give no more away. "*Your parents are dead, it is true,*" he finally said. "*But I was bidden to give you this gift, not to answer your questions. I have been far too busy sewing*"—he paused significantly, adjusting the folds of his kilt—"*to prepare answers that might satisfy you.*"

Eleni shook her head in amazement as she stared at the brooch. "I—I do not know what to say to you, sir," she finally told him, stumbling over the words.

*"Say, 'You look handsome, Brounie, and perhaps even a bit taller.' And say, 'Your stomach looks perfectly flat.' And say, 'Thank you.' And then you may tell me good-bye."*

"Good-bye?" Eleni asked. "But why should I tell you good-bye, when neither of us is leaving this place?"

*"How can you know that?"* Brounie asked Eleni, tilting his head in polite inquiry.

"Well, *I* am not going anywhere, except to Rubha nan Gall tomorrow," Eleni told him—though with more conviction than she was feeling, for she remembered now another good-bye, when Tonttu had taken his leave of her. "And I know you do not wish to leave Aros, either, Brounie," she added.

*"I could leave,"* Brounie argued, straightening his new shirt. *"If I wanted to, that is. There is such a thing as free will—even for creatures of my kind, twilight child."*

"Of course there is," Eleni agreed quickly.

*"But I will never leave,"* Brounie said. *"For this is my home. And it is almost time for me to show myself to the selkie's daughter. I promised her father I would instruct her when the time came."*

"The selkie's daugh—"

Brounie winked.

*"Iona,"* Eleni said, stunned.

And yet sleek little Iona was a bit like a seal, she realized—with her shiny black hair and her expressive brown eyes. So they were something like sisters, after all! For the blue men had said the selkies were her honorary kin. "Iona's mother was a seal?" she asked, thrilled.

"*Iona's* father *was a seal,*" Brounie corrected Eleni. "*And her mother was a lovely lass who lived on Eilean nam Ban, the little 'Island of the Women' just off the Ross of Mull. Across from the holy isle. The selkie shed his skin, you see, and walked on the island as a man for a bit, because he loved the lass.*"

"And then Iona's mother learned she was carrying his child," Eleni whispered, familiar now with the way these stories so often progressed.

Brounie nodded. "*And when the lass's father found out, he beat her, but she would not say who sired her child. But when the hour came for her to deliver, there was trouble, trouble, trouble. And by the time the selkie heard what was happening to his beloved, the pretty little lass was dead from the birthing—though Iona had been born. With 'broken flippers,' as the selkie told his friends.*"

"So what did he do?" Eleni asked.

"*Why, he shed his skin and came ashore again,*" Brounie told her. "*And he stole baby Iona away from Eilean nam Ban, because the babe's grandfather was too cruel for the selkie to leave her there. He knew she would stand a better chance in life were she to be discovered at the abbey, so he swam her over to the holy island and left her wrapped safe and warm in his very own skin. And that meant he could never go home again, Eleni, for a selkie needs his skin to return to the sea. Such was his sacrifice! For the selkie lost his love, his baby, his home, and his life all in the same day.*"

"He could have raised Iona himself," Eleni said, scowling. "He certainly knew how to fish, after all."

"*Aye,*" Brounie said, nodding. "*Only his heart was broke in two, Eleni. He died soon after kissing baby Iona good-bye at the abbey. He walked straight into the sound and kept on going. The seals barked for days, they were so sad.*"

"You must tell her, Brounie," Eleni whispered. "Iona thinks no one loved her, and that she was thrown away."

*"In time,"* Brounie said serenely. *"But I am trusting you to leave the telling to me, for that was her father's wish. As for you, Eleni, you will be too old a girl from now on to need help from a wee one such as I."*

"I will never be too old for that," Eleni protested. "Please, Brounie—promise you will still come visit, even after I have turned sixteen."

*"I canna promise you that,"* the brounie said sadly, preparing to leave. *"There will be others like me, though, wherever you go. If you need us, that is."*

"But I need you now, Brounie! Pray, do not say good-bye to me."

*"Then I will say 'farewell,'"* the brounie told her, his voice fading. *"And I hope you do fare well, wherever you go, twilight child. For you are to be our voice."*

"I told you, I am not going *anywhere*," Eleni cried, but she was speaking to an empty room.

# Chapter Twenty-One

# At Bloody Bay

"This arrived very early, by messenger," Iona said, bounding into Eleni's bedroom first thing the next morning. "Take it out of its basket! It's from Matias, see—and it's a bonnie wreath for your birthday, made of midsummer flowers."

"Bad Iona, to ruin the surprise," Eleni scolded sleepily. "You already looked?"

"I had to," Iona told her, bouncing up and down on Eleni's bed. "You said Matias told you he might put spiders in your hair, didn't you? Or dump a bucket of cold water on your head?" she asked, not waiting for an answer. "I could never let such a thing happen to you. Oh, put it on!"

"*Shhh*. I will," Eleni said, and she placed the wreath upon her tousled curls.

"You look just beautiful," Iona said, clasping her hands under her chin. "Come see," she called over her shoulder, and Moira, Bethie, Annie, and Pol slipped into the room from the hallway where they'd been hiding.

"Think of all the trouble Matias went to! These flowers are from all over the island," Moira said, straightening the delicate wreath on Eleni's head. There was golden woadwaxen, with its silky leaves, and fuzzy-stemmed blue comfrey, which Eleni knew Dr. MacReady and Matias used often when treating the islanders' various ailments, and blue forget-me-nots, their tiny yellow centers seeming to wink birthday greetings, and lavender, in honor of the name Miss Dundonald had given Eleni.

"And he made it so nice," Pol added, her eyes wide with admiration.

Eleni longed for a looking glass. "But why didn't Matias give me the wreath himself, on our picnic?" she wondered aloud.

"Because he's going to be late," Iona reported, still bobbing up and down on Eleni's bed—like a wee selkie on the waves, Eleni thought, hiding a smile. "Dr. MacReady needs him this morning," the little girl continued. "But Matias sent a message to Miss Dundonald saying you and I should go on ahead, and he'll join us later if he can."

"Well! It doesn't matter to me if he is too busy to come along," Eleni said, pretending not to care. But she touched her fingers to the wreath once more, pleased Matias had gone to so much trouble—just for her.

A flower-bedecked Fancy toiled up the slope leading to the great bluff overlooking Rubha nan Gall. The hill was treeless, like much of the island, but muscled with rock, and rolling with fragrant heather and thorny gorse. The pony swayed her shaggy head as she hauled the rattling empty cart behind her, Eleni and even Iona having long since gotten out to ease her load. Fancy's wheat-colored tail nearly dragged on the ground, it was so long. Eleni watched Duddy race up the hill, then double back behind them to nip at their heels as if they were errant lambs. "Why don't you ride in the cart now, Iona? Fancy will not mind," Eleni said, thinking of the little girl's injured flipper, as Iona's selkie father had called it.

"No," Iona told her. "Fancy's tired, too, and besides, we're almost there." Iona gestured to a path meandering through the stretch of furze that spread all around them. "Here's where we cut across the hill, Eleni. *Gee*, Fancy-girl," she commanded, urging the sturdy pony to turn right. "That trail leads to the best vantage point," Iona told Eleni, "just on the other side of Rubha nan Gall. And we'll be able to look down on Bloody Bay, as well."

"Bloody Bay?"

"There was a fearsome battle there once—more than three hundred years ago," Iona said.

"This whole island is bloody," Eleni murmured, thinking of the wreck of her father's ship, and the wreck of Spain's *Florida*, and who knew how many other disasters?

"You go on ahead," Iona told Eleni in her bossy way. "But don't get too close to the edge, mind, because the wind can really blow hard on the hill. I'll bide a wee here, with Fancy." Iona leaned against Miss Dundonald's handsome cart, easing her lame foot off the ground, Eleni noticed, sorry for the little girl.

Duddy gamboled around Eleni as she made her way up a final incline to the point overlooking the entrance to the Sound of Mull. And to Eleni's right was the rubbly point of land that had finished off her father's ship a year earlier.

Had he even known she wasn't still aboard? Probably not.

A ribbon of shoreline curled away from Rubha nan Gall and curved toward the west, underneath a series of shallow ledges that dropped down to the beach. Beyond the long stretch of shore, and sheltered by a larger and much higher point seeming to hover in the distance, was the broad curve of Bloody Bay. Eleni shivered, and the wind roared in her ears. Black guillemots cried *pee-eee* as they wheeled overhead, their bright red feet tucked neatly beneath them like little pocket-purses, and gray-and-white kittiwakes shrieked as they circled in the sky.

Iona was giving her a chance to look at this haunted place alone for a few moments, Eleni realized, grateful to her young friend. And yet—she *wasn't* alone, Eleni suddenly knew, because the rough sound of excited men's voices was making its way past the crash of waves, through the wind, and over the raucous cries of the birds. Duddy began to whine and bark as he tried to peer over the edge of the crumbling bluff.

"Whack 'em good when they fly over," a hoarse voice floated up from the beach. "They'll tumble to the shore, and then we'll bag 'em."

"I will," a nearer voice answered.

It—it sounded like Col Hardie! But where could he be?

Eleni backed slowly away from the edge of the bluff. She did not want to see Col, and she most especially did not want Col to see Duddy, the dog he had once left to die on Sgurr Dearg. But Duddy was wild with curiosity now, and he ignored her furiously whispered commands. Still gripping his fur, Eleni turned and waved her free arm wildly at Iona, who was busy combing Fancy's forelock with her fingers. *"What is it?"* Iona called out, but her voice was nearly snatched away by the wind.

*Help,* Eleni tried to say—but with a gesture, rather than a word. She pointed down, attempting to tell Iona silently that Tobermory's wildest young men were hunting nearby. But *what* were they hunting? There would be no sport in going after kittiwakes or guillemots, Eleni knew. Those birds populated the island in such numbers that it would be like—like hunting field mice or humblebees to go after them.

"Here they come," Col's voice called from underneath the bluff, and out flapped two or three dozen of the most wonderful birds Eleni had ever seen. The birds cried out in alarm as they were rousted from their snug hillside burrows, whirling up into the air like confetti at a village fair.

They were puffins, Eleni knew at once. They had long black wings, blazing white chests, dangling orange feet, and big heads—sporting triangular beaks nearly again as large. These beaks were edged in the same bright orange as their webbed feet, but they also contained vivid splashes of an amazing greeny-blue that took Eleni's breath away. It was the exact same color as the Minch itself; she was sure of it. Not sky blue, but the unearthly color of deep water at the foot of a dark, dark cliff.

Duddy was so excited by the unexpected appearance of these odd creatures that he could not stop barking. He danced back and forth along the crumbling bluff as if he were caught at the end of a fishing line. Eleni crept back to the edge and looked down.

*Whack!* A small puffin flying several feet below her was knocked out of the air by Col's long stick, and then another tumbled to the shore—to the waiting figures below—and then another fell, and another.

Some birds plummeted straight to the stony beach, knocked senseless by the blows, while those with broken wings fell in spiraling circles, their other wings flapping uselessly. A few injured puffins landed in the water, where circling seals—selkies!—awaited them, seemingly desperate to help. But those living birds who fell injured onto the beach were instantly stomped dead by the waiting men.

It was another slaughter at Bloody Bay.

The young men on the beach shouted out their laughter and waved their arms in triumph, encouraging Col to flush out additional puffins from their burrows in the bluff. "Here they come," Col shouted again, and a few more puffins tumbled into the air.

And *whack!* went his stick.

The pitch of Duddy's angry bark rose even higher. His blue eye flashed in the afternoon sun.

"Stop that, Col Hardie!" Eleni cried, leaning over the edge of the bluff as far as she dared. "Stop it, *please.*" Where her courage came from, she did not know. From her birthday brooch, perhaps, which she'd pinned to her petticoat where no mortal could see it. Or maybe her courage had been given to her a year earlier by the blue men of the Minch, who had spared her life and bidden her to protect the puffins. The blue men had led her to her safe haven in Tobermory. To her home. She must thank them in some way, Eleni thought—even if it meant saving only one puffin from this horrible fate. The birds were relying on her!

Col poked his head out from under the crumbling ledge just to the left of her, and he peered up, surprised. A slow grin spread over his red, excited face. "Why, it's Miss Eleni Lavendyre, who I've been asked not to call upon," he said, sounding both bitter and sarcastic. "And she's wearing bonnie flowers in her hair." Eleni moved back from the edge a little and touched her wreath with cold fingers. "And there's her useless lapdog, as well," Col added. *"Rowf!"* he shouted, making a sudden threatening gesture at Duddy with his stick.

Duddy hunched down and growled, and Eleni grabbed hold of his ruff again so he would not try to leap down upon Col— and possibly tumble to the beach below. *"Please* do not hurt the birds, sir," she called down to Col. "They did you no harm."

"'Course they haven't harmed me," Col said, sneering his disgust at such a remark, however accidentally insulting it might have been. "But we can sell 'em for stew, can't we? To the poor folk of the island?"

"But—it is not right to kill the birds this way," Eleni objected. "It is too easy for a fine hunter like you," she added, trying to flatter Col. "And you have all the money you need. The poor folk, they have other things to eat."

That was true. For this, at least, was a fat year on the isle of Mull.

"'Course they do," Col said, laughing. "But this is fun! *Beg me*, if you want me to stop, Miss Lavendyre. Go ahead, lassie— make it worth my while," he added, attempting to tease her in his clumsy way.

It was the manner in which some young men joked with the girls they liked after church, Eleni realized—but about littler things, such as snatched bonnets or dropped gloves, not about slaughtering helpless, beautiful birds for no reason. As usual, Col Hardie had gotten things wrong. Eleni almost felt sorry for him.

"Give me a chance, at least, to please you, Miss Lavendyre," Col said, suddenly pleading, as his teasing slipped away for a moment. "You'll find I'm not so bad, lass."

A heartbeat later, Eleni felt a frantic tug at the back of her shawl, for Iona had crept up behind her. "Don't listen to him, Eleni," the little girl whispered urgently. "Come away at once, or those men might harm us. We're all alone up here!"

"It is only Col Hardie, Iona," Eleni whispered back. "And he's clinging to the side of the hill."

"Who else is up there?" Col bellowed, embarrassed and angry that some unknown person had overheard his heartfelt plea to Eleni. He craned his neck so he might see. "Is it Miss Dundonald, who said I may not call on you? Or is it the crippled child?"

"Miss Dundonald never meant to insult you, sir," Eleni said, trying to block Iona from Col's view. "But I am too young yet to have a man come calling."

"Not in these parts," Col scoffed. "And if you're too young, then why is the Finnish lad always stopping by Aros? Answer me that," he said. He was becoming angrier and angrier as he spoke.

*Col knew of Matias's visits.* There were no secrets in a place the size of Mull, Eleni realized—or possibly on an island of any size, for that matter. "Matias is an old friend from my village in Finland, that is all," Eleni told Col. "He is like a brother," she added. Then, as if Col might be able to tell who had given it to her, she quickly removed her birthday wreath and handed it to Iona, who jammed it onto her own shining head.

"Go away, Col Hardie," Iona called out, her fear—and possibly Matias's wreath—making her brave, if only for the moment.

"Shut your gullet, cripple," Col shouted back. "I think the cripple and that useless dog make a perfect pair," Col said to Eleni, turning cruel once more. "Why, Aros is a haven for *all* the island's rejects, isn't it?"

"Do not dare talk about my home that way," Eleni said, her fury overcoming her fear.

"And don't *you* dare tell me what to do or say," Col shouted angrily. "I'm the factor's son, *Miss Lavendyre*, and I'll be factor when my father dies. I do as I like on this island. Always! And you will remember that one day, I swear it."

It was Akseli all over again, Eleni thought, chilled. What had she been thinking, to soften even a little toward this angry man? For he would never change.

"Come away," Iona urged Eleni once more, and this time, her heart pounding with fear and rage, Eleni obeyed her young friend.

"That's right, go," Col shouted after them. "And take your poxy dog with you, or I'll be knocking *him* into the sea, too. I'd like nothing better," he added, his angry voice seeming to follow Eleni, Iona, and Duddy as they hurried down the slope to where patient Fancy was waiting with their cart.

A wobbly circle of surviving puffins—Eleni's second birthday wreath—flew high over their heads in the midsummer sky, but Eleni was the only one to notice them.

She lifted a shaking hand to bid them farewell.

## Chapter Twenty-Two

*Chapter Twenty-Two*

### Saying Cruel Things

It was just after noon when Eleni and Iona neared Tobermory, their picnic untouched. Iona rode in the clattering cart while Eleni and Duddy walked alongside. "Col Hardie wanted to throw Duddy off the cliff like my mother and father tried to throw *me* away," Iona said suddenly, the look of sadness on her face matching the now-drooping flowers of the wreath.

Eleni was shocked into momentary silence by the little girl's comment. She'd been sworn to secrecy by the brounie, but she had to say something to make Iona feel better. "No, Iona," she finally protested. "We do not know what happened when you were born. And someone cared about you enough to wrap you in a sealskin, don't forget."

"That's true," Iona said, but then her brown eyes filled with tears. "Perhaps my mother and father simply didn't want to bother raising a lame child. A *cripple*," she said, repeating the harsh word Col Hardie had used, as she tried to blink her hot tears away. "And one day, no matter what you say, I'll be all alone."

"But—but no one is a finer girl than you, Iona," Eleni whispered, reaching up to take one of Iona's cold hands in her own. "Everyone loves you so much! Miss Dundonald says you are like a daughter, does she not?"

"Yes-s-s," Iona admitted, smiling a little.

"And does not Dr. MacReady love you, too? And Duddy? And Bethie and Moira and Pol love you, Iona. And so does Mrs. Lochiel. And so do I. You are *not* alone in this world."

"*Hello-o-o,*" a voice called to them from down the hill, and after a few moments Matias appeared, riding Dr. MacReady's second-best horse. "I'm sorry I am late, fine ladies. Did I miss the celebration?"

"Matias," Iona cried. "Eleni's birthday picnic was ruined by Col Hardie, up on the bluff," she said, wiping away the last of her tears.

"It was spoiled more by the sun beating down so hard," Eleni added, fanning herself with her hand and trying to laugh, for she did not want Matias to be angry with Col. No good could come of that, she told herself firmly.

"But Col Hardie said such cruel things to me, Matias," Iona persisted, not wanting to let her grievance go. "And he frightened Eleni, and he said he would knock Duddy off the cliff!"

Duddy barked sharply, remembering.

"Oh, he did? Brave lad," Matias said, narrowing his eyes as he glanced up the stony trail the cart had just descended.

"Please do not go up there," Eleni begged Matias in Finnish. "Col has many of his friends nearby, and it was not as bad as Iona said. Col was angry that he was told not to come calling at Aros, that's all."

"*That's all,*" Matias echoed, scoffing. "So Col Hardie does not need to apologize to anyone, ever, no matter what he does, Eleni? Because he has you—and everyone else on this island—to make excuses for him?" he said, his face almost without expression. "That proves my point! What I told you about Scotland being a bad place to live just now is true."

"But you said it was the English who were ruining things here," Eleni argued. "And Col Hardie is not English."

"You're right," Matias said, scowling. "But power and money can corrupt anyone, Eleni, so it comes to the same thing. But it was 'not so bad' up there with Col, you say. Perhaps Mull is the perfect place for you after all!"

"Matias," Eleni cried. "How can you talk like this to me?"

"What are you two jibber-jabbering about?" Iona asked Matias, wild with curiosity.

"Calm yourself, little Iona," Matias said to her in Gaelic. "I was just telling Eleni how pretty that wreath looks on your head, though I made it for someone else."

"Oh," Iona said, touching the wreath she'd forgotten was there. "But Eleni only gave it to me to wear because—"

"He has left us, Iona," Eleni said softly. "So there really is no need to explain."

# Chapter Twenty-Three

༺৩৩৩৩৫

# Stuck

Matias stayed away from Aros for the next three weeks, which of course made Eleni want desperately to see him again. She had lost him once, then found him, then lost him again, and she missed him.

The July weather was extraordinarily fine, which meant Miss Dundonald's washhouse was especially busy. Bethie talked to herself under her breath, trying to remember each small task that she was assigned. Moira flung linen sheets and towels over the myrtle hedges as if she were casting fishing nets into the sea. And Iona, when she could escape from her studies, tapped the end of her goose feather pen against her chin and cast her gaze upwards, trying to keep the laundry's job list accurate.

When she was finished with her own studies, Eleni floated among the different washhouse chores as though dreaming, she was so distracted by her confusion and her sorrow. She sorted laundry until her head buzzed. She worked the dolly peg until her arms burned with fatigue. She scooped pure white apple-wood ash into a barrel and poured boiling water onto it. And then the next day, she carefully poured the murky lye water she'd created onto fresh ashes to create a purer, stronger cleaning liquid. She dug the damp leftover ashes into Miss Dundonald's vegetable garden. She ironed Upper Tobermory's flounces and frills. And every chance she got, Eleni glanced up from her work and looked across the bay toward the village of Tobermory, hoping she would see Matias heading down Main Street—on his way to Aros.

But he didn't come.

At Tobermory's pier, *The Rambler of Leith*'s repairs were progressing. A long-jacketed man had set up a tall desk right next to the passenger ship, Eleni saw. She wondered where the ship might be going, but the truth was, no place in the world felt quite real to her anymore—not even Tobermory. And so she did not dwell upon the question.

Now the bulk of the third week's laundry was done, wrapped in tidy, lavender-sprigged parcels and ready to be delivered that afternoon. It looked as though the girls at Aros had finished their work just in time, too, because Willie the Post was saying clouds would soon fill the skies once more, turning the water in both Tobermory Bay and the Sound of Mull from blue to sullen gray. But like a stripe in an imaginary tartan belonging to the whole of Scotland, Eleni knew, a narrow band of sunlight would then gleam at the horizon separating sea from sky.

"Are you pining for something, Eleni Lavendyre?" Miss Dundonald asked Eleni midmorning as they passed on the stairs. "You look so sad, lass."

"Oh, no," Eleni said. "It is only that I feel a bit—a bit—"

"A bit same-y?" Miss Dundonald interrupted, trying to be helpful. "You need to stretch your legs, my girl. You should take our Duddy for a walk."

"And Iona, too?" Eleni asked, for one of Miss Dundonald's strictest rules was that Aros's girls did not go places alone.

"She's resting her legs for this afternoon's deliveries," Miss Dundonald said softly, glancing quickly upstairs. "Why don't you and Duddy walk to the little lake you visited before? You'll be safe enough there, with both Duddy and the fairies watching over you," she added, laughing.

"That is true," Eleni said solemnly, already wanting to be off.

"Take your shawl, for it's growing a bit chill," Miss Dundonald advised over her shoulder as she disappeared into the library. "And be back for dinner at one, lamb."

"Wait, Duddy," Eleni called out as the dog bounded down the path leading to the *lochan*. Duddy seemed to grow younger with each step as he neared the water.

Three months had passed since Eleni, Iona, and Matias last visited Lochan nam Ban Uaine, the lake of the green-clad fairies. The air around Eleni was heavy with the sound of summer insects, the rustle of leaves, the sighing of the wind, and the *plip-plop* of tiny creatures leaping into tea-brown water as they heard Eleni and Duddy approach.

"Duddy," Eleni called again as she pushed her way past a branch that seemed to have doubled in length over the last twelve weeks. But Duddy was already halfway around the lake, head down. He sniffed at the water's edge as if he had never smelled anything half as interesting in his life. "Silly puppy," Eleni murmured, taking her seat on Iona's moss-covered log. The moss felt drier today, as if it had been crisping in an oven. Eleni closed her eyes, ran the palms of her hands lightly over the moss's yellowing surface, and imagined that she was in the forest near Inkoo once more.

"Hello, *tyttö*," a gentle voice said to her in Finnish. "So you have come to this lake again, too?"

Eleni's eyelids flew open and her heart thudded. "Matias! What are you doing here?" she asked.

Matias pulled a list from the basket he was carrying. "I'm *supposed* to be gathering elder flowers to treat the rheumatics," he said, reading aloud. "And coltsfoot for coughs, and marsh-mallow for the digestion. And I'm to search out some meadowsweet for fevers, on my way home. But I think Dr. MacReady really sent me here to talk to you, Eleni. I believe he and Miss Dundonald have hatched this little plot to get us speaking again."

Eleni looked away, blushing, for she was beginning to suspect the same thing. "They should not interfere when friends quarrel," she said softly.

"And are we still friends?" Matias said, sitting down at the log's other end.

"Of course," Eleni told him. "We were children together, Matias. You are my *oldest* friend."

"And no more than that?" Matias asked, tilting his head. Flickering forest shadows played across his face, Eleni couldn't help but notice. Splashes of sunlight highlighted first his wide cheekbones, and then the strong clean line of his jaw. His dark brows made him look stern, but the expression in Matias's blue eyes was tender, and it sent a shiver up Eleni's spine.

"Oh, yes, something more than that," Eleni said, leaning forward a little. "Only—I cannot explain it, Matias," she said, turning away again. And it was true. Eleni could not find the right words to say, not in the Gaelic or English Miss Dundonald and Iona had been teaching her, nor in Swedish *or* Finnish, because she had never spoken in such an intimate way to a young man before.

And the truth was, she did not yet know what it was she *wanted* to say.

"Well, if I try to explain how I feel about you, will you do the same?" Matias asked gently, and Eleni nodded. Matias waited for a moment, then he spoke. "When I saw you again that first night in Aros, I was the happiest I'd ever been," he began. "Until you collapsed at my feet, that is," he added, laughing. Eleni couldn't help but smile.

"And the truth is," Matias continued, "I had not even known how sad I was before that day. I suppose I thought that—that simply *enduring* this life was all a person could expect. The loneliness I felt in Helsinki after my mother died, and those endless days at sea, and the quarrels and curses and shouts that surround you when you live only among men were what life was, I thought. *My* life, anyway."

Eleni held her breath.

"Oh, there were times at sea when I felt moments of joy," Matias conceded. "When there was freshly caught fish for dinner for a change, or when I heard the sound of laughter, or when the wind picked up after a long, boring lull. But that joy was nothing compared to what I felt when I saw you again, Eleni Lavendyre. I thought we had lost one another forever, you see."

Eleni turned her head so that he wouldn't see the tears in her eyes. She tried to remember how to breathe.

"I know you are still a young girl," Matias said softly, "and I do not mean to frighten you. But whenever I see you, my heart grows bigger, don't you see? It is a miracle! Your pretty face, and your green eyes, and your hair, and your hands, and—and—"

"All girls have faces and eyes and hair and hands, Matias," Eleni teased gently, interrupting him. "And I think they are meant to make men stammer. That is not a miracle."

But in truth, she understood what he was trying to say. For wasn't she feeling the same about *his* face and eyes and hands? She peeked at those hands now, so strong and brown, and scarred a little in places from his years at sea.

She pictured Matias's hands stroking her hair and caressing her shoulders.

"Are you cold, little Eleni?" Matias asked, seeing the goose-flesh on her skin.

"No," Eleni said, rubbing her shawl against her arms to erase the telltale bumps.

"So it is your turn, now," Matias said, looking uncertain for the first time since they'd met that day. "How do you feel about me?"

"I am happy, like you," Eleni began shyly. "And I feel calm when I am with you, Matias. The way I used to feel when I was alone in the forest." But she was not feeling calm right now,

Eleni thought, listening to the pounding of her own heart.

"Go on," Matias said, moving a little closer to her on the log.

"You know the truth about who I am—and *what* I am," Eleni told him softly. "Also, I do not like to talk much with most people, as you know. But I always want to talk to you. Things seem better when I can tell you about them. Even the bad things," she added. "I am at home with you, Matias."

"And yet you did not want to tell me about seeing Col Hardie on your birthday," Matias said, clearly making an effort to keep his voice mild.

"I didn't *mean* to see him," Eleni told him. "Iona and I were surprised by Col up on the bluff, but we left that place as quickly as we could. And I didn't want to tell you, because I was afraid you would go after him," Eleni said.

Matias's laugh was without humor. "As if I were afraid of Col Hardie! That stuffed and preening sausage of a lad."

"But it wasn't only Col Hardie who was up there," Eleni said, trying to explain once more. "His friends were with him. And so it would not have been a fair fight."

"You like Col Hardie," Matias said, looking away from her.

"I don't," Eleni protested.

"But you did like him, didn't you?" Matias asked, narrowing his eyes as he turned to look at Eleni once more.

Now, Eleni was the one whose laugh was bitter. "Do you mean before I came to *know* him?" she asked. "Even then, Matias, the most you could say was that I thought he might not be as bad as some people said. I felt a little sorry for Col Hardie, for he is headstrong and brash—like a silly boy who keeps wishing to do the right thing, but does not know how to go about it."

Col was like her own *isä* in that way, she thought suddenly, surprised. Perhaps her father had joined the rebellion without thinking clearly about what would happen next, certainly not to his family. And maybe he had snatched her away from Inkoo without considering the consequences of that action, either. "I will tell you a secret, Matias," Eleni said suddenly. Matias held perfectly still, and Eleni took a deep breath. "After you arrived in Tobermory and began working for Dr. MacReady, I imagined that you and I might stay together forever," she said. "And—and make our own family here, on Mull," she added, blushing.

"But then what happened?" Matias whispered.

"You told me you didn't want to stay on Mull after all," Eleni told him. "And so what am I to think of our future?"

"You would rather stay on Mull with Col Hardie than start a new life somewhere else with me?" Matias asked.

"Not Col Hardie. Never Col Hardie!"

Matias shook his head, as if pitying her. "Do you really think you will have a choice in the matter, Eleni? Even Miss Dundonald cannot protect you each hour of every day for the rest of your life, if I were to leave this place. Why, if Col Hardie had been at the lake today instead of me, what do you think would have happened?" He sighed. "It seems I cannot leave Mull, because I must protect you. I am stuck here, like—like a stag in a bog, and you don't even see it. You don't understand that we need to find ourselves a new place. A new world."

"But you are not being fair, Matias," Eleni said. "You ask

how I feel about you, and yet what good does it do me to say, if you do nothing but argue with me?"

Matias laughed, shaking his head. "Do you remember once telling me back in Finland that a Russian was a Russian, even if he was fried in butter?" Eleni smiled a little, nodding. "Well," Matias asked, "what do you think that meant?"

"I don't know," Eleni confessed, looking sheepish. "I was angry with the Russians for fighting our fathers, and I love butter, and so I said it, that's all."

"Well," Matias told her, "what the saying *really* means is that a person isn't going to change simply because he dresses differently, or speaks a new language, or lives in one place instead of another. You are my little Finnish Eleni, with all your quirks and gifts, whether you live in Inkoo, or in Tobermory, or—or somewhere else, with me."

This was almost the same thing Brounie had told her, Eleni thought, surprised. That her *gifts* were her home, and she would take them with her wherever she went. "But if it doesn't matter where a person lives, Matias," she argued, pushing the memory aside, "why not live here, where we are happy? Tobermory is my home now, but you have made it clear that you will not stay to share it with me. And so I am stuck, too."

"You just told me *I* was your home, Eleni," Matias said quietly. In a moment, he was at her side—so close to Eleni that she could feel the warmth of his body. And to her amazement, he took her face between his hands.

"Matias, no," she said softly. "We—"

But he stopped her soft objection with a kiss that was so warm and gentle it was like a Finnish summer. And yet as tender as it was, Matias's kiss stirred Eleni—enough to startle her a little. But she kissed him back before she pulled away.

Matias laughed. "Let me kiss you again, Eleni Lavendyre," he whispered. "I will stay on this island forever, if you will only let me kiss you one more time."

"You won't stay, you can't!" Eleni protested, laughing a little sadly as she curled against his chest and stroked his old leather vest. "And you *shouldn't* stay here, Matias, not if you really want to leave this place."

"But I love you to pieces, *tyttö*," Matias said, teasing the child Eleni used to be. "And you love me, too, I know you do."

"*Sir,*" Eleni objected playfully, pulling away from him a little. "I have never said so." But she wanted Matias to kiss her once more.

A sudden flapping of wings filled the air around them as Duddy plunged through the nearby undergrowth, scattering birds—pretend sheep, most likely—in front of him as he went.

"Duddy!" Eleni cried.

"*Duddy,*" Matias exclaimed in an entirely different tone of voice as the faraway village clock chimed the half hour.

"Oh! And dinner is at one," Eleni said, standing up and dusting herself off, as if in so doing she might erase any visible traces of the embrace they had just shared.

"You may go if you must, Eleni," Matias said, getting to his feet more slowly. "But I won't be far from you ever again. I can promise you that."

# Chapter Twenty-Four

# Fight!

"Hurry, Eleni," Iona said after their one o'clock meal. She sounded a little cross. "Buckle the harness. We must be off, or we'll get caught in the rain later up on the hill."

The damp weather must be causing Iona's lame leg to hurt even more than usual, Eleni thought. Either that, or Iona was angry that she, Eleni, had gone to the *lochan* without her. If she only knew what had happened there! "I *will* hurry, Iona," she replied. "But please, let Moira help me deliver the laundry today. You rest a bit more."

"Moira is sweeping the washhouse," Iona snapped, not wanting to be given any special consideration. "And Bethie is helping Pol prepare dinner tonight, because Mrs. Lochiel has gone to visit her sister down in Ardnacross. And this was part of my job before you even came here, Eleni Lavendyre, so don't tell me what to do," Iona added, stamping her foot. "Steady, Fancy-girl," she added, soothing the restless pony as a now-silent Eleni tugged at her harness, making sure it was snug.

Two hours later, although the rain had finally started to fall, a more cheerful Fancy pulled the empty rattling cart down Upper Tobermory hill. "Climb in now, or you'll slip on the stones," Eleni urged Iona, who was also feeling more cheerful. Iona complied, not wanting the folks in town—especially that nice, red-haired Angus Hume—to see her limp down Main Street.

But it was not Angus who stepped out of the shadowy doorway of the British Fisheries Society office, it was Col Hardie. Col looked as if he had spent the afternoon drinking ale in the Gull & Gherkin, Eleni thought, her palms growing cold. She ducked her head in the vain hope the staggering Col would not notice her—or, worse, somehow sense that she had recently been kissed. It seemed to Eleni that such a thing must be apparent to everyone.

Col's face was flushed, his black hair disheveled, and his clothing a little awry, as if someone had been tugging at the tails of his red jacket. Not that anyone would dare. "There you are," he said to Eleni, ignoring Iona. "I thought I saw you go by earlier, girl."

"We have been working, sir, and now we must return home," Eleni told him, still keeping her gaze cast down on the shiny wet stones beneath her feet. Iona clucked under her breath, urging Fancy to walk on, but Col grabbed the shaggy pony's harness and held her back.

Eleni noticed that in spite of the rain, a number of men had gathered to watch what was happening. They nudged one another expectantly, but no one interfered with Col. One or two of the men even looked amused, as if they wished *they* could act as bold with passing girls as did this privileged lad.

Thunder rumbled over the Sound of Mull. "Let go our pony, please, sir," Iona said, working hard to keep her voice steady, but Col ignored her. He swayed back and forth on his feet. His beefy face was dull with ale, and the rain had flattened his usually pouffed black hair so much that snaky locks lay pasted against his forehead. Irritated at being kept from her supper, Fancy tossed her head, and more raindrops went flying.

"C'mon, Col. That's enough," Angus Hume said, bursting out of his father's office.

"You spoke rudely to me t'other week, *Miss Lavendyre*," Col said, ignoring his friend. "When I was hunting puffins out at the point, remember? And I gave you every chance to be sweet. So I demand an apology. Or—a kiss," he said, suddenly inspired as he leered around at the gathered men as if seeking their approval.

"A kiss, a kiss," one of them began chanting.

*A kiss, a kiss,* Eleni thought as if in a dream, and she remembered kissing Matias.

"Stop it, Col," Angus warned. "Come in out of the rain, and—"

"Just grab her, lad," another called out. "She's nought but a strumpet, no matter what Miss Dundonald says, and you're the factor's son." It sounded like Ian Mackay, but Eleni was too frightened to look.

"Yah, but she's also Miss Dundonald's ward," another man warned. "And Miss Dundonald is a Maclean, don't be forgetting."

"Well, my fine lads," Col said mockingly, "ever since Culloden the Macleans are scattered over all the western isles, *'don't be forgetting.'* And it's my father who speaks for the laird now. Not some by-blow of his bawd of a cousin."

He was calling Miss Dundonald a "by-blow"—an illegitimate child!—in public. And he'd called Miss Dundonald's mother, the spirited Flora Maclean, a bawd. Eleni was stunned.

The onlookers clearly thought this was going too far, even for Col Hardie, for Miss Dundonald was much loved by the villagers. She had donated money to build the stone church, after all, though shunning all public acclaim. She quietly aided those fishermen's families whose men were lost at sea. She paid for poor people's costly salves and potions almost before they knew they were ill. Even Ian Mackay owed her a debt, and he knew it. Hadn't Miss Dundonald given him work at the laundry after he'd been injured fishing?

And so Ian Mackay did a quick about-face and began scowling at Col Hardie through the rain. "The girl's not so bad," he mumbled.

Sensing that the mood of the crowd had turned against him, Col's anger and boldness only grew the greater. "Come to me, lass," he said to Eleni, "and let's show them how it's done." He reached for her arm, but his hand twisted around her shawl, instead. Undeterred, Col tugged Eleni toward him.

Resisting his grasp, Eleni turned in place on the slippery stones as if she'd just been spun like a top. But this made the men start laughing again—which caused Col to become even angrier. "You mock me?" he bawled out, though Eleni could not tell to whom he was speaking.

"Col, come *on*," Angus said, keeping his voice low. "These young ladies are wanting to go home, now."

"But they *aren't* ladies, and they haven't got a home," Col shouted. "The lasses at Aros are the absolute dregs of the isles, are they not? And they're ours for the taking, Angus. So I'm grabbing *my* girl now, I swear it! And I'll teach her to treat me with respect from this day forward." He reached for Eleni once more, and this time, his hand touched flesh.

"Coward," Eleni cried out, shrinking away.

"*What* did you call me?" Col asked, unable to believe the word he had just heard.

His free arm went back, and he made as if to strike her face—hard.

And it was Matias who stepped into the fray. "She called you a coward," he said clearly, as if explaining, and he interrupted Col's threatened blow with his own upraised arm.

"Where did you come from, foreigner?" Col asked, not even looking at him.

"From a fair country that does not like bullies, redcoat."

"Don't you dare call me a bully *or* a redcoat," Col said, blustering. "I'm a gentleman, so I'm 'Mr. Hardie,' to you."

"Well, I can't bring myself to call you that," Matias said, shrugging. "But I can call you 'coward,' as Miss Lavendyre did. And I don't think there's anyone here who would argue the point, either. Interfering with two girls and a pony," he added mockingly. "What's next? Stomping butterflies? Stealing sugar-teats away from babies?"

"I'm frightened," Iona cried.

"C'mon, Col," Angus said, tugging at his friend's wet sleeve. "Let's go have another ale, and leave these folks alone."

But Col paid no attention to Angus. "Step back, foreigner," he said to Matias, still not bothering to look at him, as his eyes remained fixed on Eleni. "She's *my* girl. You'll have to wait your turn. But don't worry, I'll tire of her before long."

"You just made a mistake, redcoat," Matias told Col calmly.

Her old friend sounded almost . . . happy, Eleni realized, chilled.

Thunder boomed overhead as Matias's muscled arm went back, and his fist flew through the air and connected with Col's jaw. And the fight began. Col was soft from spoiling, though, and Matias's hard life, coupled with his years at sea, gave him the clear advantage. The onlookers who had not sought shelter from the storm in the public house cheered and booed, almost at random. Beside herself with worry, Eleni clasped her hands and tried to stay out of the way.

"*Hup, hup,*" Iona said, trying to control Fancy, who had been made nervous by both the storm and the fighting men, and was pulling to get away.

"Let her go, young miss," the gallant Angus called out, leaping forward to steady the pony. "She'll know the way home from here, I'll wager."

And so the pony cart went clattering off down the wet cobblestones in a gentle *S,* toward the lane leading to Aros. The rain was coming down in sheets now, falling so hard Eleni could barely see what was happening in front of her own eyes. But she did not move from where she stood.

"Help me! Hit him from behind, men," Col bawled, hunching over as he tried to cover his face, of which he was extraordinarily proud.

"This is *our* fight, redcoat," Matias shouted, glancing over his shoulder to see if he was about to be swarmed. But he was not, for those few men who remained standing outside in the downpour were not pained to see a powerful Hardie—any Hardie—finally get a beating. And Col was being bested in this fight. A flash of lightning illuminated the street for a moment.

"Knock him down," Col yelled into the rain, still bent over and covering his face. "Knock him down for me, lads, and then I'll finish him off. Angus, where are ye? Anyone? I'll *pay* you to hit the foreigner for me!"

"Do it yourself, coward, if you think it's such a good idea," Matias shouted, positioning himself to throw another punch, should Col ever straighten up long enough for them to continue the fight.

"Matias, stop," Eleni called out. "You'll get in trouble!"

"I don't care. Look at this worm, Eleni," Matias shouted in Finnish. "This is the creature who insulted you!"

"Dirty foreigner," Col cried. "*Take* the little wench, if you want her so much. Here, I'm giving her to you!" He reached for Eleni.

Soaked to the skin, Eleni drew back, shocked.

"She's not—yours—to—give," Matias said, punctuating his words with blows to Col's well-padded ribs. Matias was furious now—at every cruel and unfair thing that had ever happened to him and Eleni, in Finland *or* in Scotland.

"I'll kill you, foreigner," Col howled, clutching his side with one arm as he scrabbled crablike across the wet stones. "I vow it! If I had my knife on me, you'd be a dead man right now."

"What, stabbed in the back?" Matias said, landing another thudding blow. "With others being paid to hold me down?"

"I'll do whatever it takes," Col said, almost sobbing out the words.

"Matias, stop," Eleni begged again, reaching out her hand.

"See how she tries to touch him," Col shouted. "And she always acted so proper and pure," he jeered, straightening up long enough to give Eleni a shove.

Eleni stumbled backwards on the slippery stones, but she quickly righted herself.

"Another mistake, redcoat," Matias said, sounding almost like a schoolteacher correcting a wayward pupil. And his fist flew through the air once more.

"Help, help," Col cried through blood, clutching at his jaw. "You've knocked out a tooth, foreigner!"

"So now," Matias replied, panting, "whenever you see your gappy smile in the looking glass, you can remember this day— and what happens when you insult a fine young lady."

"She's nought but a bawd, and I'll have my revenge on her, too—long after you're gone from this island!" Col cried, springing toward Matias. It was as if he had suddenly realized he was alone in this battle, and no one, no matter how much he offered to pay them, was willing to come to his aid.

And so he might as well fight.

Eleni forced herself to watch as the two young men fell to the cobbled pavement, rolling back and forth on the gleaming stones. Col's hands were around Matias's throat one moment, and he pulled the young Finn's hair the next, but Matias countered the panicky young man's every undisciplined move.

And soon, Matias had Col pinned on his back in a puddle. Rain pelted down on Col's face, and he gasped like a fish just landed. "I'll kill you," Col managed to shriek once more.

And then, as if she were trapped in a terrible twilight dream, Eleni saw Col's flailing hand connect with a loose cobblestone some carriage wheel had knocked aside. Col's fingers gripped the stone as if this was his last hope to win the fight, which it was.

And Eleni was powerless to stop him.

Slowly, as if it were happening underwater, Col's arm came up—and he bashed the stone down hard on the back of Matias's head. Eleni heard the *crac-c-k*.

"No!" she cried out as Matias rolled senseless onto his side. She threw herself on the ground and crawled toward Matias, intending to block any further blows with her own body. For what was life worth if her beloved Matias was dead?

*"Yes,"* Col mumbled hoarsely, struggling to his knees. In a moment, he had straddled Matias's barely moving body and was using both shaking hands to raise the red-shining cobblestone over his head once more. He looked at Eleni. "Watch this, *Miss Lavendyre*," he said to her through smiling, bloodstained lips.

He was going to bash Matias's brains out.

## Chapter Twenty-Five

# Duddy's Revenge

B efore Eleni could react, a ball of black-and-gray fur came hurtling through the air. It was an animal, and its ears were pinned flat against its skull and its lips were drawn back in a fearsome snarl.

Fancy must have found her way back home, Eleni realized instantly, and Iona cried out for help, and Duddy had come racing to the rescue. His blue eye shone like a shooting star as he flew past Eleni's head—and then the dog was all over Col.

This was to be Duddy's revenge upon Col Hardie.

"Matias!" Eleni cried, rushing over to her bleeding friend. Matias groaned, his return to consciousness aided by the pelting drops of cold rain that spattered his bloody face. He touched a bruised hand to the back of his head, then looked at his palm as rain washed the blood away. *"Uh-h-h,"* he groaned.

"It's a wolf!" Col was screaming. "Help me!"

Eleni turned her head just enough to see the bloodied cobblestone tumble from Col's hands as Col tried to push away the dog.

Col was in no real danger, Eleni realized almost at once. If Duddy were trying to rip out the young man's throat, the deed would already be done. Instead, Duddy was merely punishing Col—and buying Eleni enough time to rouse Matias and flee.

Another clap of thunder seemed to shake the very air around them. The skies were black with the storm now, and a cold blue wind swirled in from the sound, almost knocking Eleni sideways. "Wolf, wolf!" Col shrieked again as Duddy mangled the famous scarlet jacket and nipped at Col's arms while he tried to cover his face. But there was no one listening to him, because the last drenched onlookers to Col's fight with Matias had fled inside the red door to the Gull & Gherkin's warm, smoky comforts.

"Up, Matias! You must try to stand," Eleni said urgently in Finnish.

Matias struggled to his knees, clutching one hand to the back of his head. Finally, finally, he staggered to his feet and stood swaying as he watched Duddy wrestle with Col Hardie. "We—we cannot leave the dog behind," he said to Eleni.

And hearing those few words, Eleni knew for certain that she would love Matias forever. She gave him her heart.

"Mama," Col howled, and he pulled what was left of his red jacket over his head and struggled to his feet.

Duddy gave one last snarling growl, his head sunk low and his ruff raised high with menace. The gentle sheepdog *did* look a little like a wolf, Eleni thought, backing away with her protective arm circled around Matias's lean waist. "*Psst,* come," she whispered to Duddy, trying to get the dog's attention. The storm's din muffled her command, but Duddy glanced at her for a fraction of a second. And that was all the time it took for

Col Hardie's booted foot to shoot forward in a vicious kick aimed at Duddy's heaving ribs.

And *that* was all the time it took for Col's other foot to skid out from under him. He flipped in midair, and he came down hard, banging the side of his head on one of Main Street's shining stones. He lay crumpled and still in the pouring rain. Duddy whined uncertainly, and he trotted to Eleni's side.

"Oh, no," Eleni murmured, hiding her eyes with a shaking hand. Duddy leaned into her, afraid for the first time.

"Eleni, Matias, come away with me at once." Miss Dundonald's voice cut through the storm. "You must escape to Aros."

Beside her, a rain-bedraggled Iona was wringing her small white hands.

"No, Meg," Dr. MacReady's voice cut in. "There will be no shelter for them there. Not if Col Hardie is dead." And he knelt to examine the lad.

"But—but we did nothing to make this happen," Eleni cried out into the storm. "Col challenged Matias, and they fought, and then Col fell!"

"That is not how the story will be told," Miss Dundonald told her. "Folks may respect us here, but Jamie and I can only do so much to protect you."

Dr. MacReady looked up from Col's side. "The boy lives, but he is badly injured. And who knows what condition he'll be in when he awakens?"

"Oh," Eleni said, newly horrified.

Col could be cruel, but his last word had been "Mama," after all. In this one way, at least, Eleni thought, Col was like all other folk. He was like Pekka, who had hung scarecrow-like in the cold black Northern Sea. Col was like herself, when she'd wept for her mother onboard the *Saari*. Perhaps Col was even like her own father, when his ship went down off Rubha nan Gall. Isä might have called out "Äiti" in his last moments, too. People cried for their mothers at the end.

"They will say that Matias bashed him with that stone," Miss Dundonald said, pointing to the glistening cobblestone Col had brought down on Matias's head.

Dr. MacReady narrowed his eyes in thought. "Take them to the pier, Meg," he told Miss Dundonald suddenly. "They must set sail for the new world on *The Rambler of Leith* this very night, storm or no storm. Bring them there. Tell the captain to assemble his crew—but on the sly. Say that I will sneak aboard in an hour or so and straighten out the details of the passage. And then return to Aros quickly, my dear. You are too easily recognizable to risk letting anyone see you near the ship."

"But Jamie, the *Rambler* is not to sail for another two—"

*"Go,"* Dr. MacReady urged his old friend. "I've heard that the ship has already been loaded, and the gold will take care of the rest. What better way to spend a bit of it, Meggie? But hurry now, and stay hidden as best you can," he urged them. "People will be venturing out soon, and then the search for Matias and Eleni will begin. I'll stay here and tend to Col. Go, I say! And take Duddy with ye."

"But—where's Iona? I cannot leave without her," Miss Dundonald said, looking frantically around.

"I'm staying with Eleni," the little girl cried, her voice shrill.

"All right," Dr. MacReady agreed hastily. "We can fetch Iona home later, Meg. Now, scoot!"

# Chapter Twenty-Six

## The Rambler of Leith

*The Rambler of Leith* was still pulled alongside Tobermory's one pier, ready to set sail in two days' time. Many eager people had signed on for passage, spurred by both the promise of a fresh start and by the worry that the Clearances would soon spread further to the western isles.

"Hurry," Miss Dundonald said, herding Eleni, Matias, Iona, and Duddy down the swaying pier as if she were the sheepdog now. "And watch your step, mind. These boards are slick with rain."

As if anyone needed to be reminded to take care after what had happened to Col, Eleni thought, numb with cold and fear.

"Ahoy the ship," Miss Dundonald called out hoarsely, approaching *The Rambler of Leith*. The trim ship rose and fell in the heaving waters of Tobermory Bay.

To Eleni's surprise, the ship's captain was aboard that night, despite the fierceness of the storm. He emerged from his cabin and peered over the ship's side. His glance was sharp and knowing as he summed up in a moment what was obviously a critical situation, for these remained turbulent times in Scotland. "Come aboard. Take shelter," he said in English, pointing toward his cabin door.

"It's just these two who need your help," Miss Dundonald told him, gesturing toward Eleni and Matias. "Dr. MacReady will be along shortly to tell you what you need to know—and to pay you for their passage. Pay you exceeding well," she emphasized, leaning forward. "But sir, you must gather your crew now, and quietly. Tell no one what is happening!"

The captain nodded once, to show that he understood exactly what she was saying to him. He reached out to help an unsteady Matias climb aboard his ship.

Eleni made as if to follow him, but Miss Dundonald took hold of her hand, tugging her back, and Duddy circled the girl's wet skirts and whined his distress. "Wait a moment, lambie," Miss Dundonald said softly. "We won't be seeing each other again, you know. Not in this world."

"No," Iona cried, clinging fast to Eleni as the rain slicked her black hair down shiny and smooth.

Eleni sank to her knees. "You must be brave, *sisar*," she told the little girl. "You *will* see me again one day, I promise. But you know I may not stay here now, so it is you who must give Miss Dundonald and Duddy my love each day. Do you understand?"

"Yes," Iona said, sobbing.

"And you will still have a good friend at Aros," Eleni whispered in the little girl's ear. "His name is Brounie, and he has been waiting to make himself known to you. He has something wonderful to tell you, Iona—but more than that I cannot say."

"Really?" Iona whispered back, her brown eyes wide.

Eleni nodded, then rose to her feet. "Oh, Miss Dundonald," she said, flinging herself against the woman's cushiony chest— her *"misdundundun,"* Eleni thought suddenly, almost laughing and crying at the same time as she remembered her first botched lesson in speaking the Gaelic.

"You must be a brave girl, now, Eleni," Miss Dundonald told her, as Duddy leaned hard against Eleni's trembling legs. "But what am I saying? I know what a courageous lass you have been in the past—especially at sea."

"But if I can be brave from this day on," Eleni said, her tears mingling with the rain, "it is only because you made me so. With your love."

"Lambie," Miss Dundonald exclaimed. "You've made *yourself* brave. You will see that one day."

"I have been so happy at Aros," Eleni said, sobbing as she hugged the big woman who had taken such good care of her. "Oh, life is hard!"

"It is indeed," Miss Dundonald said, and then she held Eleni at arms' length. "Now listen to me, Eleni Lavendyre," she said, lowering her voice to near-whisper. "Jamie will be bringing you enough gold so that you can do as you please in the new world, at least for a time. *Alone*, if you so wish it. You're to make a life with Matias only if it suits you, do you hear me?"

Eleni nodded, eyes wide.

"But if it does suit you to marry Matias, do not say no, as I did to Jamie," Miss Dundonald said softly, sadly.

Eleni nodded again. "I will not. And I will remember all about Tobermory and Aros, Miss Dundonald. And—and I will tell my children the story, too. All about you, and Dr. MacReady, and Duddy, and the girls, and especially my dear little sister, Iona. And I will tell them about Tonttu, and the blue men, and the fairies at the lake, and the selkies and the puffins, and about Brounie, too. Oh, say good-bye to Brounie for me, will you? He watched over me all the time I was here!"

Miss Dundonald nodded, smiling through her own tears.

Eleni sank to her knees one last time, and she pulled a shivering Duddy close. "Brave boy. I thank you for everything, my darling Duddy," she murmured into the trembling dog's wet fur. "I thank you for your blue eye, and for your kisses, and for your little snores, and for all the love you gave a lonely Finnish girl."

Frantic and whimpering, Duddy tried to lick her tear-stained face, but Miss Dundonald tugged him gently away. "We three will hurry home now, Eleni, and you and Matias must hide onboard the ship until it leaves. The townsfolk are beginning to venture out," she whispered, tilting her head toward the distant doorways. Slashes of light had begun to shine on the little town's wet black street. And in a moment, Miss Dundonald, Iona, and Duddy were halfway down the pier.

The captain poked his head over the side of the boat once more. "Come aboard, miss," he said to Eleni. "Your young man is injured, and he needs you."

"Good-bye," Eleni called out into the cool Scottish night.

"But I cannot accept such a gift from Miss Dundonald," Eleni whispered to Dr. MacReady half an hour later, after the doctor had cleaned and bandaged Matias's wound. "Not after what she's done for me already." And she pushed two small but surprisingly heavy leather bags back across the captain's table.

"You must take the gift, or she'll have my head," Dr. MacReady said softly, laughing. "There's enough gold left to last Meggie a hundred lifetimes, never fear. And I'll be here if she ever runs short. But don't ye be showing these old coins around willy-nilly, or saying where you got them, even in the new world," he warned Eleni. "It's a secret, mind. The captain has been paid in English money, so he won't be asking any questions," he added, winking.

"But—but sir, how did Miss Dundonald come by such riches?" Matias asked, staring at the two heavy leather bags.

Eleni's eyes grew wide. "It's the gold from the old Spanish wreck, isn't it?" she said, nearly breathless.

Dr. MacReady didn't utter a word, but his eyes twinkled in the lamplight.

Matias shook his head, amazed. *"Aros, oro,"* he said suddenly. *"Oro* is the Spanish word for gold, you know."

"That neat coincidence wouldn't surprise me one little bit, son," Dr. MacReady said softly. "Nor would it have surprised Flora Maclean or young Meggie Dundonald. They always said it was a valuable thing to learn to dig a garden."

"So the gold was in the ground at Aros for all those hundreds of years," Eleni said, thrilled.

"I'm not saying another word," Dr. MacReady said, dropping another wink as he prepared to leave them.

"You—you called me 'son,' sir," Matias said to the doctor, suddenly shy.

Jamie MacReady smiled at him. "I told the captain that's

who you were, and I said your name was Matthew," he confessed. "I said you were a freshly minted doctor looking to get away from a spot of trouble here. And I told the captain you were called Ellen Lavender," he added, turning to Eleni. "It'll be easier for you both in the new world to have English names. I hope you don't mind."

"I'm honored," Matias said, bowing slightly.

Above their heads, Eleni heard the familiar sounds of sailors getting ready to cast off. These men were quieter than the *Saari*'s sailors had ever been, though, because this ship's midnight departure was to be a stealthy one. "Dr. MacReady?" Eleni asked suddenly.

"Yes, my dear?"

"Will Col Hardie live?"

"He will, after all," Dr. MacReady reported, nodding. "He was regaining consciousness when I left him, though he kept muttering, 'Wolf, wolf.'"

Eleni smiled, much relieved. "Then he may not blame Duddy for what happened to him," she said.

"He won't blame Duddy at all, just as he'll never find either one of you," the doctor confirmed. "In fact, he'll probably tell folks that the fairies spirited you away at his command, to save face."

"But will he trouble you or Miss Dundonald, do you think?" Matias asked, worried. "After all, Eleni lived at Aros, and I was staying with you."

"Oh, the factor may get riled and make a show of looking for you two once he returns to Tobermory," Dr. MacReady said. "But that'll be over soon enough. No matter how much his son pesters him for revenge, the factor won't be forgetting it's the Macleans who give him his power on this island, and Meggie Dundonald is a Maclean, after all. And if I might say it, Mull needs its best doctor."

Eleni smiled. "Dr. MacReady?" she said once more, though more shyly this time.

"Yes, lass?"

"Ask her again."

"Beg pardon?"

"Ask Miss Dundonald again. To marry you, I mean," Eleni said, hardly daring to believe that she could speak such bold words. "Her answer may have changed."

And Miss Dundonald's answer *would* be different this time, Eleni knew.

"Really?" Jamie MacReady said, a blush creeping above his whiskers.

Eleni nodded.

"Well, then," Dr. MacReady said. "Well, then, I believe I might. She's the sweetest lass I ever met, and a fine figure of a woman, too."

"You will find a new world of happiness," Matias told the doctor, though it was Eleni he was smiling at. And Eleni smiled back at Matias.

She was home.

# Epilogue

# 1794

# New Scotland

Ellen Lavender and Matthew MacReady were married at sea by the captain of *The Rambler of Leith* on the second of August, 1794, some two hundred miles east of Nova Scotia. "New Scotland," the celebrating sailors called their destination, and Eleni knew that she and Matias would be happy there. Matias would be a doctor—a bone-setter, a gash-stitcher, a fever-soother—as he had always wanted to be. And her own useful purpose would soon be made clear to her. Eleni was certain of this.

The bonnie ship was surrounded by frolicking harp seals all during the brief ceremony, and Eleni was certain the blue men of the Minch had bid them come to serve as witnesses to the celebration.

"Thank you, friends," she whispered to the spotted seals.

Instead of a bridal dress, Eleni wore the simple gown in which she'd last delivered Miss Dundonald's laundry and a wonderfully wrought brooch made of three precious metals, centered by a stone the color of Matias's eyes. A single ribbon of ruffled sea grass twined through her shining hair. More than one hardened sailor was so moved by her beauty that he wept.

And no two people ever had a happier or more enchanting wedding.

⊗

*"Look after them, O fair God
keep them, steadfast Creator
and keep them out of harm's way
guard them from all ills
lest they come to grief. . . ."*

The Kalevala

# Author's Note

The idea for *Twilight Child* began some twenty years ago, near Inkoo, Finland, although I didn't realize it at the time. I wasn't even a writer yet; I was a visual artist, and my younger son and I were invited to what seemed like one of most foreign places I could imagine for a monthlong stay. In between all the drawing and sightseeing, however, I became increasingly fascinated with both Finland and the Finns. Luckily for me, my well-informed Finnish friends had answers to every wide-ranging question I could dream up—then, and during another monthlong stay two years later. A recent visit confirmed my love for this beautiful country and its people.

A year after I first visited Finland, I visited the Scottish island of Mull—alone, and almost by chance. I didn't know anyone there at all, and though I'd gone to Mull to draw, I found myself buying local maps and dictionaries that proved useful to me when I began work on *Twilight Child*. It was as if I were already planning to write the book all those years ago! I fell in love with the island for many reasons and was greatly impressed by the sense of history that is still so alive there.

Not a day passed when I didn't hear "the Gaelic" spoken, for instance, or listen to a still-bitter account of "the Clearances." I found Mull to be a heartbreakingly beautiful place, and I longed to stay there—or at least to return.

When I began writing fiction, Finland and Scotland began resurfacing in my mind as possible places to write about, each having made such a strong impression on me. At first, the idea of combining them in one historical novel was a little like putting hot fudge on ice cream: I loved them both, so why not? But later, I discovered that it also made historic sense, as there had been much exchange between the two regions for so many hundreds of years.

When I began doing general research for the book, however, I found further reasons to combine the two, as political parallels between the two countries grew apparent to me. In fact, I began to see the 1790s as a period of great change for large numbers of people—including the fictional Eleni, who learns to survive and remain herself throughout a time of social upheaval and ends up fleeing to "the new world," as so many of our American ancestors did.

Since *Twilight Child* is a novel, and not a history book, much of my research is, I hope, invisible. However, I think that many people would be interested in knowing more about that period, so I have included some historical information below, for curious readers. Further notes are available on my Web site: www.sallywarner.com.

In 1787, Finland was under the control of Sweden, then a great power in northern Europe. The Swedish army was at war with Russia, and the Finns were caught in the middle. Sweden and

Russia continued for years to struggle for control of Finland. After defeating Sweden in the war of 1808–1809, Russia annexed Finland as an independent grand duchy. Finland did not become independent from Russia until 1917.

Meanwhile, Scotland was attempting to recover from its own war with mighty England. This war had ended in 1746 at the brief and bloody Battle of Culloden, when Scotland was defeated.

After conquering the Scots, the English did everything they could to establish their rule over Scotland for all time. The English decided they could make more money by raising sheep than by farming in Scotland, and so, to make room for sheep to graze, the lands were cleared of the people and small farms—"crofts"—that had been operating there for centuries. Crofters were driven from their homes, often by extremely brutal means. Many Scottish families fled to North America at this time. This dark period, which went on for many years, is referred to as "the Clearances."

Mull is a large island off the west coast of Scotland. Its many standing stones, stone circles, and crannogs (ancient loch dwellings)—dated to about 2000 B.C., the Bronze Age—make it clear that the island has been settled for thousands of years. Much of the population of Mull was erased during the Clearances, however.

The Macleans have been Mull's leading clan for hundreds of years, though they lost their castle and lands to Scotland's Duke of Argyll in 1691. All references to them—and to the Dundonalds—in this book are completely fictional, as are all references to Aros.

Tobermory, the largest town on Mull, is situated at the

northern part of the island. Tobermory was founded as a village in 1788 by the British Fisheries Society, but there was a settlement there much earlier than that. "Tobermory" means "the well of Mary," and it was called that as early as 1540. One of the ships that left Tobermory for the new world during the Clearances was, in fact, *The Rambler of Leith,* which sailed for Nova Scotia in the summer of 1794, as it does in *Twilight Child.*

Iona is a very small island off the southwest coast of Mull. This tiny and reputedly holy isle has its own special place in Western history, being said to be the burial place of many Scottish kings and chiefs, including the Macbeth of Shakespeare's play. It was also the home of St. Columba—who brought Christianity to Scotland—until he died in the year 597. The ruins surrounding St. Columba's abbey still stand, and the abbey itself has recently been restored.

In spite of the Christian history of Mull and Iona, many of the Gaelic place names on the island reflect the islanders' former pervasive beliefs in such supernatural beings as fairies, brounies, and enchanted selkies, among other creatures. This is reflected in the real "Little Lake of the Green-Clad Women," to use its English translation, though I changed the lake's location in *Twilight Child.* Likewise, all references to Finnish sauna trolls, fairies, and other woodland spirits are, I believe, accurate to the time.

"The Minch," the passage between the Inner and Outer Hebrides, has served as a shortcut through those islands for centuries. It is a very dangerous stretch of water and is also referred to as "the current of destruction."

There are several different explanations for the long-standing belief in the tribe of supernatural sea creatures known as "the blue men of the Minch." While they were considered by some to have been fallen angels or the northern descendants of Glaukos, a godlike creature from Greek mythology who was half fish, more recent speculations include the possibility that the original blue men—if they existed—might have been abandoned Viking captives, either African or heavily tattooed.

Finally, laundry practices in the 1700s were complicated, time-consuming, and very expensive, due mainly to the cost of fuel. While the depiction in this novel of such practices is essentially accurate, it is also sketchy and lighthearted. Doing laundry was extremely strenuous work, taking days out of every week in most prosperous households and up to ten percent of every budget.

Women were eager to have outside help with this chore, of course, but there was a fear of mingling one's family clothes and linens with those of unknown strangers. This fear gradually was overcome, and more laundries—such as the one romantically described in *Twilight Child*—came quickly into being.

# Pronunciation Guide
## (and some definitions)

## FINNISH

**Names of people:**

Ahti: AH-tee (ancient god of the deepest sea)
Äiti: EYE-tee (mother)
Akseli: AX-sell-lee
Eleni: ELL-any
Isä: EE-sah (father)
Jakob: YA-kob
Matias: MAT-ee-us
Pekka: PECK-kah
Simo: SEE-moh
Väinämöinen: VAY-neh-moy-nen (ancient sage of the
Kalevala)

**Names of places:**

Helsinki: HEL-sink-kee
Inkoo: IN-koh
Lågnäs: log-NASS (this is a Swedish word for a Finnish
place; it means "shallow cape")

**Other Finnish words:**

Juhannus: YOU-ha-noos (Midsummer)

**Kalevala:** KALL-eh-va-lah (ancient Finnish epic poem)
**keijukainen:** KAY-you-ky-nen (fairy)
**kiitos:** KEE-toes (thank you)
**kiuas:** KEE-oo-ahs (raised ovenlike structure in the middle of an old sauna)
**koira:** KOY-rah (dog)
**lemmikki:** LE-mek-kee (forget-me-not flower)
**menninkainen:** MEN-en-ky-nen (larger forest creature)
**peikko:** PAY-koh (forest troll)
**pulla:** POOL-lah (sweet bread)
**ruiskukka:** ROO-ees-kocka (blue flower that grows in rye fields)
**sauna:** SOW-nah (heat room; also used for bathing in old days)
**saunatonttu:** SOW-nah-tahn-too (sauna troll)
**savusauna:** SAH-voo-sow-na (smoke sauna)
**sisar:** SEE-sar (sister)
**sisu:** SEE-sue (courage)
**tonttu:** TAHN-too (troll)
**tytär:** TOO-tare (daughter)
**tyttö:** TOO-tuh (girl)
**valkovuokko:** VALL-koh-voo-oh-koh (wild anemone flower)
**ystävä:** OOS-sta-vah (friend)

## SWEDISH

**flicka:** FLEE-kah (girl)
**fru:** FROO (ma'am)
**ja:** YA (yes)

nej: NAY (no)

Svendgard Wallibjörn: SVEND-gard WALLY-byorn

## SCOTTISH

Gaelic: GOLL-ick (pronunciation in western isles; a language)

Names of people:

Brounie: BROW-nee

Dundonald: dun-DON-ald

Iona: eye-OH-nah

Lochiel: lock-EEL

MacReady: mick-REED-ee

Moira: MOY-rah

Names of places:

Aros: AH-rose ("large house at the mouth of a river")

Culloden: kull-AH-den (Scottish battle site in 1746)

Eilean nam Ban: eye-LEEN nam BAN ("island of the
women")

Hebrides: HEB-reh-dees

Iona: eye-OH-nah (the place)

Lochan nam Ban Uaine: lock-en NAM ban WAYNE ("little
lake of the green-clad women")

Mull: MULL ("maol" = blunt height; "meall" = mound)

Rubha nan Gall: roo-BAH nan GALL ("point of the
strangers")

Sgurr Dearg: s'gurr DEERG ("high red hill")

Sruth na Fear Gorm: srooth NAH fear GORM ("stream
of the blue men")

Tobermory: TOW-burr-more-ee ("well of Mary")

## OTHER WORDS FOUND IN *TWILIGHT CHILD*

**ghillie:** GILL-ee (male attendant to a laird)

**guillemot:** GIL-ly-mot (bird)

**kittiwake:** KIT-ty-wake (bird)

**laird:** LEHRD (Scottish clan chief)

**Lavendyre:** LAV-en-deer (in England, 14th century: a woman who laundered clothes; in Old French: "lavandiere" = laundress; French and Middle English "laund" = lawn or pasture where washed clothes were laid out to dry)

**Leith:** LEETH (an area near Edinburgh, in Scotland)

**Sassenach:** SASS-en-ack (Scottish put-down for Englishman)

# Acknowledgments

First, I thank Mirja Kivistö and Juha Karhu for their warm hospitality at Lågnäs during my three stays in Finland. I also thank Mirja for her research into eighteenth-century Finnish names. In addition, I thank her for everything she taught me about Finnish history during the twenty years—so far!—that we've been friends.

Mirja is one of the most rational people I know, and so I appreciate especially her forbearance in answering my repeated questions about various Finnish supernatural beings. Any mistakes I have made, whether historical or otherworldly, are entirely my own.

I wasn't even writing books when I last visited Mull, that beautiful and memorable Scottish island, so I thank Tobermory's Donald Kirsop for his generous help in answering my long-distance questions about the history of that town's streets and churches. Although many of the events referred to in Part Two of the book are based on historical fact, I have taken considerable liberties in several areas. Among them are the depiction of

1790s life in Tobermory, which was not then as large a town as I've made it out to be; the complete fabrication of Dundonald family history—including their tartan; of Aros's history; of Maclean family history; and of the history of Duart Castle, which was out of the Macleans' hands between 1691 and 1910; and the change in location of "The Little Lake of the Green-Clad Women," one of Mull's smaller lakes. If, in addition to these intentional fabrications, I have made other mistakes, they are my own.

I also thank my South Pasadena neighbor Maaret Toprakci and her daughter Kristi for helping me with Finnish spelling and pronunciation. Again, any mistakes are my own.

Finally, I thank Phil and Robin Wright for giving me *Forgotten English*, which informed *Twilight Child* in numerous ways and with several entries, but especially with one evocative word that inspired the entire book: "lavendyre."

Sources I am indebted to are:

*Forgotten English*, by Jeffrey Kacirk. New York: William Morrow and Company, 1997.

*The Kalevala: An Epic Poem after Oral Tradition*, by Elias Lönnrot, translated from the Finnish with introduction and notes by Keith Bosley. Oxford: Oxford University Press, 1989.

*Sea Room: An Island Life in the Hebrides*, by Adam Nicolson. New York: North Point Press, 2001.
Nicolson's stories about the blue men of the Minch and

his vivid account of an 1850s cliffside puffin hunt were very helpful to me, as I missed seeing Mull's puffins by one week when I was bird watching. And—thank goodness—I missed seeing the blue men entirely!

*Boswell's Life of Johnson*, volume V, by James Boswell and Samuel Johnson, edited by George Birkbeck Hill, D.C.L. New York: Harper & Brothers, 1891.
This entertaining book provides a look into eighteenth-century Mull and life in the Hebrides.

*The Highland Clans: Their Origins and History*, by L. G. Pine. Rutland, Vermont: Charles E. Tuttle, Inc., 1972.

*Laundry Bygones*, by Pamela Sambrook. Buckinghamshire, U.K.: Shire Publications, 1983.
This illustrated English booklet provides a thorough look into the history of laundry and ironing practices.

*The Placenames of Mull*, by Duncan M. MacQuarrie, M.A. Inverness, Scotland: John G. Eccles Printers Ltd., 1982.
A reader can get lost for hours in this fascinating book in which Mr. MacQuarrie translates all of Mull's names from Gaelic into English.

**SALLY WARNER** is the author of many highly acclaimed novels, including *Sort of Forever* and *This Isn't About the Money*. She and her husband live in Southern California with their miniature wirehaired dachshund.

For more information about Sally Warner and her books, please visit **www.sallywarner.com**.